DOCK OF THE BAY

DOCK OF THE BAY

Written by

Linda Lynch-Johnson

2018

Copyright © 2018 by Linda Lynch-Johnson

All rights reserved.

Names and persons in this book are entirely fictional. Any resemblance to actual persons, living or dead, or actual events is purely coincidental.

ISBN 10: 1727216415
ISBN 12: 9781727216417

Library of Congress Control Number:
2018910805

Printed in the United States of America

Dedication

To my dear, loving husband, Rob, this book is dedicated to you. Without your presence in my life, I would not have had the courage to pursue my dreams! My sons, Robb and Stephen, their supportive spouses and their amazing children, and my loving siblings whose presence in my life I value so much, remind me every day of how blessed I am!

Chapter One

The first time Bailey Stephens heard Otis Redding singing "Dock of the Bay," she was driving over to Golden Gate Park with the top down on her old 1952 Ford convertible - it was its permanent position - and the salty air of the San Francisco Bay was filling her lungs. The DJ was announcing that this was the last song Otis Redding recorded before his tragic death in a private plane accident in December.

That old Ford didn't have much, stripped down and cheap, but the lack of the canvas top that converted it into a sky arena made the tears in the upholstery and the musty smell from the radiator leak last winter, worth it. The view through the windshield held misty hills as the car crossed the Golden Gate Bridge. The smells of exhaust from the buses intensified, but that day held clear, winter crispness that was magic. How could it be otherwise, with the music turned up to overcome the traffic sounds and that haunting voice of Otis? He got it. He understood our Bay. Any Bay area native could tell by the way the words made them feel.

Saturday afternoons in Golden Gate Park were filled with musicians, artists, kids throwing footballs and Frisbees, the "flower children" that gravitated to the Park and couples walking hand in hand. San Francisco and its park were a dichotomy of hippies, anti-war protesters and the staid native San Franciscans that went back generations,

When the seasons changed, it was just a gentle meld from one to another with only the outer clothing providing a few more layers. The subtle whiff of pot blended with the scent from the pine needles crushed underfoot as Bailey made her way over toward the Japanese Garden; it was 1968 and the park bordered on the Haight-Ashbury area of San Francisco.

The Japanese Garden was an oasis within the park, a place to sip tea and try to maintain your balance when you made your way over the steeply arched bridge that drew visitors and natives alike. It remained a haven, a place of contemplation. The garden would be full today, it was warm for February.

However, Bailey wasn't here to sip tea, but to meet a new client. She was a private investigator, newly licensed by the State of California.

She didn't take the normal PI route – as former law enforcement-turned-private-eye, but, instead, it was through community college courses- after realizing that being an attorney wasn't in the cards – too many books with too many "wherefores" in their pages. Days and nights in some dusty law library getting paid peanuts, working 80-hour weeks so that the partners could drive Jags and Mercedes, not going to happen.

It was while interning at the law office that Bailey first met A.J. – one of the investigators. That was it. No doubt that was the path to take. Bailey hung on his every word, soaking up the language, ignoring the case work and asking question after question. A.J. tolerated her questions, but just barely.

That's my kind of freedom, Bailey thought. Spending time with the investigators the firm hired was much more exciting.

Chapter Two

This new client had been referred by a former law school buddy, Peter Simmons. He had stayed the course and was going to be clerking for some judge over the summer. Seems the new client was in some kind of jam but didn't want to talk over the phone so they arranged to meet at the Japanese Garden.

"How will I know you?" he asked

"I'm the one with jeans, a paisley shirt, fringed leather jacket and long, red hair," Bailey answered. "How will I know you?"

"I'm the one in the suit."

"Okay, I don't know what you've heard, but not everyone dresses like a hippie. I do it to blend in, but suits are still pretty common, especially at the Japanese Garden."

"But it's a park."

"Yeah, but its San Francisco. I take it you're not from around here?"

"Los Angeles, okay? I'll have a trench coat on and I'll be carrying a satchel. Shouldn't be too many of those in the park. Look, enough talk on the phone, I'll tell you more when we meet."

Bailey almost repeated the San Francisco line again but didn't want to alienate the client so early in the relationship.

"Works for me. By the way, my name is Bailey Stephens, you being all private and everything, you never even asked. I could have been anyone calling."

"Nope. Peter said you had the sexiest voice he ever heard, and I'd know what he was talking about as soon as you said 'Hello.'"

Thank you, Peter, she thought. Not a great way to start a professional assignment, but she'd heard that all her adult life.

"Yeah, well, I'll see you at 1 pm on Saturday at the garden. Not hard to find, just follow the signs or ask someone. See you then."

Chapter Three

Theo Rizzoli showed up at the San Francisco Airport, as instructed. He held the photograph of Carl Younger he had brought with him and began to match it to each male passenger as they exited. He threw his cigarette out the window of his car and pulled in behind the cab that Younger hailed.

This Younger fellow was pretty big, not at all like he envisioned an accountant; the only thing even a little bit "regular" was the glasses he kept pushing up. The guy looked like he could be playing linebacker for the 49ers. But Theo was no midget himself. This job would be no problem. Still, he wondered why he was sent to do it. There was plenty of talent in Frisco to handle this kind of a job, but hey, he didn't care, the money was good, and he always liked an excuse to eat at Alioto's at the wharf.

Younger didn't pull off in town, so scratch him meeting anyone in the city. Theo followed the cab as it took a roundabout way to the entrance to Golden Gate Park. There were a lot of offices around. Maybe this was the place. But no, the cab pulled over at one of the entrances to the park and Younger got out.

Theo pulled into a parking space and exited his car before Younger could pay the driver. He followed him into the park and saw him enter some oriental garden place. He didn't know what this guy was up to, but his orders were clear: don't let him out of your sight and get any information he has. Quick and clean, then get out of there.

Chapter Four

Earlier that day, Granger Williams was parked at the curb of the Arrivals terminal at San Francisco Airport in his gray rental car.

He saw Younger get in the next cab in line while he pushed his glasses up on his nose and held his satchel close to his chest. Granger pulled in behind the cab. The target wouldn't be looking for anyone following him in San Francisco this soon.

Granger drove up from Los Angeles the night before, as soon as he had been told that Younger had booked a flight to San Francisco. He decided to leave his car in long-term parking and rent a different car. This gray Mercury was different enough that Younger shouldn't get suspicious.

Younger coming to San Francisco was a red flag for his client. He had been given strict orders to note who he talked to and where he went.

He noted the medallion number of the cab, in case they got separated in traffic, but traffic was light that morning. The noontime traffic hadn't started yet. It was an easy ride north up Highway 101. He pulled over into the right lane, expecting the cab to exit as they approached the city. But the cab went right on by all the usual exits. He was puzzled. Where was this guy going?

They were almost to the Golden Gate Bridge, when the cab exited toward Golden Gate Park. Maybe, his client had it wrong? Maybe this trip had nothing to do with Younger's work and had some romantic meaning, instead. Nah, he saw how protective he was of that briefcase.

Soon, the cab dropped Younger off at the 8th Avenue entrance to the park. He exited the cab, leaned back in and said something to the driver, nodded his head and headed into the park.

It was midweek, so Granger didn't have any trouble pulling into a parking spot at the curb. He left the car and followed; pulling a camera out of his bag and stopping now and again to take photos, while discreetly also photographing Younger.

Chapter Five

So, there Bailey was, walking into the garden, looking for this guy in a trench coat.

Bingo! There he was, pushing his glasses up off his nose, pacing and looking hard at everyone who entered through the gate.

"Where have you been? It's freezing out here!" He wiped his nose on the handkerchief he pulled from his pocket.

She turned back and looked at the clock at the entrance. It was just chiming at 12:45 pm – she was never late – one of her only "good" traits according to her father - and the radio said it was 60 degrees, warm by San Francisco standards.

"Alright, then, let's start walking. And your name is?"

He glanced around. "It's Carl, Carl Younger."

"All right then, Carl, what can I do for you?"

"Everything we talk about is confidential, right?"

"Right. So, answer my question."

He reached into his satchel, pulled out a manila file folder, shoved it into her hands, and snapped the case shut.

Bailey glanced at the tab on the folder. It was labeled Gleason and McKinney. Her head jerked up. That was the name of the law firm where she had interned.

"What's this all about? Where did you get this?"

He pulled out his handkerchief and wiped his nose, glanced around again and looked at his watch.

"Yeah, okay, I'm an accountant for Hughes and Klein in Los Angeles. I was doing an audit prior to a merger handled by that law office. Something didn't jive. I knew Peter worked in San Francisco and asked his advice. Look, just read the file. Your retainer check is inside. It's a cashier's check – not easy to trace. I have to get back on the plane to L.A. before anyone knows I'm gone."

"How do you know Peter?"

"We were fraternity brothers at the University of San Francisco before I transferred to UCLA."

"Hey, how do I get in touch with you?" she called out to him as he ran back toward the exit.

"Peter. You can call Peter."

Bailey walked over to a bench and opened up the file. Wow, that was some retainer check! Five-hundred dollars. She wondered what Peter had told him about her rates.

What she read changed everything. Her knowledge of the inner workings of the law firm confirmed that what she held was extremely confidential and, if true, would bring down that old, revered firm of Gleason and McKinney.

Chapter Six

Michael Allen, the “Son” in Allen and Sons, was about to negotiate a huge deal for his company - a buyout of Swift Investments.

His firm had put forth an order to purchase Swift Investments many times but had always been refused. Andrew Nelson, the owner and CEO, wouldn't even consider any of the "invitations" offered by several of the top companies on the West Coast. Allen was apprehensive about the sudden deal. There were too many “red flags.” This offer didn't come from Nelson; it came from no less than Stan McKinney, a partner in the law office of Gleason and McKinney, one of the most prestigious law offices in San Francisco.

Even though his firm was in San Francisco, the financial audit was being done by a firm in L.A.

Even more puzzling to Allen, was that the price accepted was dead-on the last offer—no negotiations, no attempt to raise the price and with a fast closing as well: as soon as the financial audit was finished. Now, Allen wasn't one to look a gift horse in the mouth, but he also followed the adage: "If it seems too good to be true, it probably is."

Granger Williams was a private detective and had done some L.A. work for Allen's company before. Allen had good rapport with him, so it was only natural that when this investigation was needed, Allen would call Granger.

The job seemed pretty straightforward: find out who the auditor was and make sure he or she didn't have any connections with Swift Investments or the law firm, Gleason and McKinney.

Chapter Seven

Carl Younger always had a knack with numbers. He was fascinated with the simplicity and the way everything always worked out in the end: he always found the penny.

From the time he was a boy, he kept track of every cent he was ever given or earned. His family always said that he'd always have the first penny he'd ever gotten.

That made him a whiz in math, but not so popular with the other kids; they just wanted to copy his homework, or even pay him to do theirs. When he refused, there was no room at the lunch table and no one to speak to either.

Each school year found him more and more isolated as his grades continued to be A's and even his high school teachers couldn't challenge him anymore. He attended college on scholarship by the time he was sixteen.

Carl could do all the maths: calculus, trigonometry, statistics, but he loved the simplicity of accounting. The formulas were perfect, and he wasn't fodder in a lab somewhere.

Meeting Peter Simmons at the University of San Francisco changed things for Carl. Peter was taking a forensics accounting class for his pre-law degree and they both decided to pledge a new fraternity catering to academic scholarship. At first, Carl was dubious, but Peter was also special with a flawless memory, and it was the first time Carl felt a part of something that was even remotely mainstream college life.

Chapter Eight

Carl went on to get his master's in accounting at UCLA, while Peter stayed at USF for law school. They kept in touch even after Carl had relocated to Los Angeles and went to work at prestigious accounting firm of Hughes and Klein.

Because of Carl's genius with numbers, Hughes & Klein handed him their most sensitive audit cases. They became the "go to" firm for major film studio clients and handled many of their personal accounts as well.

It was not uncommon to receive a referral from an out-of-town client such as the law firm of Gleason & McKinney. Greg Hughes had known David Gleason for a number of years and they always managed a round of golf when either of them was visiting the other's city.

McKinney, Gleason's partner, wanted to use a local accounting firm that he knew, but Gleason said he wanted Hughes's best accountant to handle the audit and, as he was the senior partner, McKinney backed down. So, it was assigned to Carl Younger.

Chapter Nine

Carl worked long hours and was frequently still at his desk when the night security guard started his shift. The guard, Tom, would pass by Carl's office and see neatly stacked reports on his desk. Everything about his office reflected his meticulous need for order.

Carl didn't look like your stereotypical accountant. By the time he was eighteen, he stood over 6'4" tall, had a football player's build and nobody would have kicked him off the lunch table just by looking at him, but his demeanor was shy and he had a habit of pushing his glasses up on his nose with his left index finger; that almost got him in trouble once, because a jock in class thought he was giving him the finger.

It was as though the gods have played the ultimate joke: a hunk of physicality and a self-effacing demeanor.

When Hughes assigned the audit to Carl, he told him that it was crucial that it be completed promptly as the terms of the buyout had a time limit to them. Carl nodded, "I'll take care of it."

That was enough for Hughes. Over the few years that Carl had been working for him he never failed to meet whatever timetable was requested. Hughes had seen him work 12 to 14-hour days to bring an audit in on time. In truth, Carl didn't have a social life, so he looked forward to these kinds of challenges.

Carl separated all of the financial reports into separate piles: one for Allen and Sons, the other for Swift Investments.

He read the financial papers and knew that these were two of the biggest players in San Francisco. Swift Investments had a select client list of old money; Allen & Sons listed some of the top public entities among their clients. Carl didn't understand why Andrew Nelson, whose client list consisted of the "A" list of San Francisco, wanted to sell. And why now?

But it wasn't his job to figure out "why" any client wanted to do what they did. That was up to Hughes or Klein or one of the other partners to counsel ramifications. He'd seen a lot of strange mergers and hostile takeovers since coming to the firm.

About four days into the audit Carl noticed something. All the accounts seemed to tally, but some of the companies that Swift was investing in weren't listed on the stock exchange. Sometimes investors put money into start-ups, but that hadn't been Andrew Nelson's strategy in the past.

Allen & Sons' financials were easy to track. Everything was in order and the books were streamlined and trackable. Not so with Swift. Carl couldn't find any record of three of them, but because they were filed in San Francisco, he didn't have access to research them further, and he didn't feel like he could sign off on the financial audit until he had more information. He made an appointment to meet with his boss, Greg Hughes, the next morning. Carl put them in his briefcase before leaving so he'd be ready for that meeting.

Chapter Ten

Carl walked over to the boss's office with the files he compiled as soon as he got in. Hughes's office was in the back corner with a view of Griffith Park. Carl didn't know how anyone could get anything done with that view. His own office didn't have a window, and he had requested it like that. As he moved up in the firm, he was offered another office, but said the one he had suited him just fine.

Hughes's secretary, Anne, was outside Hughes' door with a fresh cup of coffee waiting to take into her boss. She noticed Carl approaching.

"Oh, no, didn't you get my message? Mr. Hughes had to reschedule. Anything I can do for you, Carl? He had an important client fly in last night and they are meeting in fifteen minutes."

Carl didn't like confrontations and, to be truthful, he had a bit of a crush on Anne, so he apologized and asked her to tell Mr. Hughes it was very important that he speak to him before the end of the day.

Carl went on to his office and set the files down on his desk, but something wasn't right. He kept his current working files on the right-hand side of his desk and completed files on the left. They had been switched and were messier than when he left them last night. He had given strict instructions to the cleaning crew that they could clean the rest of the office, but his desk was off-limits.

He picked up the phone and dialed.

"Maintenance."

"This is Carl Younger. Did you hire any new cleaning staff?"

"No, Henry is still cleaning your floor, why was there a problem?"

"I'm not sure; could you have Henry stop by my office when he gets in?"

"Sure, Mr. Younger, I'll take care of it."

Chapter Eleven

Carl hung up the phone. He carefully transferred the piles over to the correct side and proceeded to start work.

He stopped and looked at the top sheet of the Swift/Allen audit and saw that the referring attorneys were from the firm his friend Peter Simmons had interned for a year or so ago.

Carl decided to call Peter. They hadn't talked since their fraternity reunion. He needed someone to do some legwork for him up in San Francisco and Peter was connected. He looked up his work phone number, dialed and asked for his extension.

Peter picked up after six rings. Yes, Carl had a bad habit of counting things: steps to the water cooler, rings of the phone, mundane stuff like that.

"Hello, this is Peter Simmons, how may I help you?"

"Hey, Peter."

"Carl! How are you! Still at that firm in Los Angeles?"

"Still there. I've got a quick question."

"Right in the middle of reviewing a case, so can't talk long."

"I won't take long. You interned at Gleason and McKinney, right?"

"Yes, a while back. Are you thinking of switching professions?"

"Never! I like my numbers. Black and white. Listen, I'm handling an audit and I need someone to do some research for me in San Francisco. I'd prefer someone with legal expertise, if possible. Your firm hires private investigators, right?"

"I know just the person, Bailey Stephens. She's in demand, but she owes me a favor. Do you want her number?"

"That would be great, thanks, I really appreciate it. If we both weren't so busy we could take in a 49'ers game someday, huh?"

Peter laughed and gave Carl Bailey's phone number.

Carl decided that he didn't want to make this call from the office; he would wait until he got home.

Chapter Twelve

Henry knocked on Carl's doorjamb. "Mr. Younger, the maintenance manager said you wanted to see me?"

"Thanks for stopping by, Henry. When you cleaned last night you didn't do my desk, did you?"

"Oh, no, Mr. Younger! You've told me don't touch the desk, so I don't touch the desk."

Carl smiled, "Thanks, Henry, I do appreciate that. Just one more question, did you see or hear anyone around my office last night while you were cleaning?"

"No, sir, I didn't, but I was polishing the marble near elevator banks, so that machine is pretty noisy. Can't hear myself think."

"Okay, thanks for stopping by, Henry."

"Sure thing, Mr. Younger and anytime you *do* want me to clean that desk of yours I'll put a shine on it like a mirror. I've got some polish that does just the trick!"

Henry moved on, whistling to himself. He didn't know what was going on, but he couldn't take any chances until he could meet with Mr. Hughes.

Throughout the day Carl continued to check with Anne. She said there just wasn't any room on Mr. Hughes calendar that day but to stop by first thing in the morning and she would try to move something around.

Carl packed up the files and notes he was working on to take home.

Chapter Thirteen

When Granger Williams started in the private investigation business, he purchased as non-descript a car as he could find. And the winner was: a tan Oldsmobile Starfire sedan.

Allen called him later that day to say the audit had been handed over to an accountant named Carl Younger. That helped. Now he had an actual target to tail. Granger's first morning was recognizance: get a lay of the land, the hours and who came and went.

The description of Younger was pretty specific and it didn't take long for Granger to narrow it down. His target was a real go-getter—first one in, last one out. He watched the night security guard lock the door for Younger long after everyone else had left.

There was a lot of traffic on the street in front of the Hughes and Klein Accounting offices, right off Wilshire Boulevard in the Miracle Mile. Parking places were hard to come by and there was a strict policing of meters and chalking of tires. Granger had to be on the lookout for his next parking place and jump on it before he lost the spot.

The following lunchtime, he noticed Younger go down to the corner deli, grab some food and a container of coffee then head back into the building. He figured he'd need some background on this guy. Younger held the door open for a cute, perky blonde who exited with her skirt exactly at knee length—apparently the regulation of every professional office in the district—no mini-skirts in sight. But Granger smiled as she hiked it up after exiting the building; walked with a sway of the hips and entered the same deli Younger had just left.

Granger guessed she was waiting to be discovered for the movie star she imagined herself to be as she sashayed into the deli. He knew Younger wasn't going anywhere right now, so he fed the parking meter and made his way in right behind her.

After ordering a cup of coffee, Granger leaned back and watched the blonde. It didn't take long for her to notice him eyeing her. She pushed her hair behind an ear and looked up and smiled.

Chapter Fourteen

Granger Williams was not hard on the eyes, he'd been told, and he never had any trouble connecting with the opposite sex, but the best advantage that a PI had was being able to blend in and not be too memorable. But he could make a dimple in his right cheek appear when warranted, and he used it now.

He asked if he could share her table.

"There's lots of empty tables."

"Really? I didn't notice."

She smiled and waved her hand to the unoccupied seat across from her.

"Why is such a pretty girl having lunch alone?"

She giggled, "I'm not anymore."

"I'm Granger."

"Monica."

"Work around here?"

"Hughes and Klein."

"Modeling Agency?"

Monica tilted her head, "Accounting."

"No way! I can't imagine anyone that looks like you being stuck in some office."

"It's my day job. I take acting classes at night." She flashed a proud smile at him.

Just as he figured.

Monica loved to talk about herself and Granger found getting her to stop was harder than getting her to start. He needed to get back to his stakeout, but he knew she'd be a wealth of information.

"I'm going to be in this area for the next couple of days. How about we meet for lunch tomorrow?"

"Well, I guess a girl has to eat."

Chapter Fifteen

Later that evening Granger followed Younger home. He noticed that Younger was taking a different route than he had before, making sudden turns and whizzing through yellow lights. Granger slowed down and pulled back. He knew where he was going, so there was no need to tip his hand.

He stopped for gas and then made his way over to Younger's bungalow in Pasadena. There was his brown Buick parked in the driveway and the lights were on inside.

Granger parked his tan Starfire behind Younger's neighbor's black Dodge and away from the street light. He was still trying to figure out how Younger had spotted him, when the front porch light turned off and the front door opened. Younger looked up and down the street. Granger slumped down in the driver's seat and glanced up through the windshield. Okay, it was official. Younger was spooked about something.

Chapter Sixteen

Granger met Monica for lunch the next day and with very little prompting got the full rundown on everyone who worked for the firm. She even mentioned Younger and how "stand-offish" he was and didn't even notice when a girl was giving him the eye, but the biggest piece of information was that he had suddenly asked for the day off.

"What's so strange about that?" he asked.

"Well, he *never* asked for a day off on such short notice and wouldn't even say why. Like I said, weird."

Something was up. Granger stuck around until Monica had to get back to work. He decided to stand around outside his car and see what Younger might be doing. He used the building's window across the street to track the reflection of anyone entering or exiting the accountant's building. Younger came out, glanced around and made a beeline for the travel agency up the street from his office.

Granger waited. Younger came out about 15 minutes later and re-entered his office building. Then Granger made his way over to the agency.

"Excuse me? Did my friend come in yet? He's tall with blond hair and glasses?"

"Why, there was a man just in here that fits that description. Is there a problem?"

"Oh, no," Granger smiled, "I was supposed to meet him here, to make sure we were scheduled on the same flight. Which flight was that again?"

"Let me see, I was just entering the information into the system. Oh, yes, tomorrow morning Flight 168 on United to San Francisco and returning the same day. Is that the one?"

"Oh, thank God! I thought he hadn't gotten my message about the change of plans, but it looks like he did. Originally, we were coming back the next day. Whew! Thanks so much for your help!"

"Of, course, glad to help. Do you need a ticket?"

"No, thanks. My company books it for me."

Granger went down to the payphone on the corner and called his client, Michael Allen, collect. He explained what was going on and asked him if he wanted him to go to San Francisco himself.

"Absolutely! I want you meeting that plane and letting me know where he goes and who he meets with. Call me with the details when you get up there."

"Got it."

Granger went home, quickly packed an overnight bag, stopped by the bank, filled the tank with gas and headed north up Highway 101 before the traffic got crazy.

Chapter Seventeen

After following the cab from the airport Granger held back as he saw Younger enter the Japanese Tea Garden, then picked up a map of the Garden and looked at his watch, like he was waiting for someone.

Younger looked around and then started talking to this tall red-head in a fringed jacket. At first, he thought he was asking directions, himself, but then saw them start to walk off together. He pulled out his camera and started taking pictures. He knew Younger had contacts in San Francisco. He had attended school at the University of San Francisco for his undergrad degree, according to the background information he had compiled on the guy.

Maybe it was romantic. He could see himself getting involved with someone like her. That hippie garb didn't disguise her curves and that red hair was a definite attraction magnet.

Younger had his back to him as he leaned in to talk to the girl, continually glancing around. He handed her something and the girl visibly paled. She got in his face and spoke intently to him. Younger immediately got up to leave and shouted something back at the girl.

Granger felt himself poked by an elbow as a group of school kids rushed the entrance. By the time he turned back, Younger had disappeared.

Chapter Eighteen

Just after hearing the clock chime 12:45, Theo was starting to go through the gates when he saw Younger start talking to some tall, redhead. Hey, maybe a little romantic something, "monkey" business. He chuckled to himself, pulled out a pack of cigarettes, shook one out and lit up.

Just as Theo was throwing down the match, he watched Younger give the redhead something that looked like a file folder. The redhead didn't like it and yelled at him. Younger walked away and called something to her. Theo couldn't hear as some school kids in uniforms came pushing through the gates. He barely had time to get out of the way and not lose Younger in the crowd.

He'd take care of Younger and find out what was in that folder and who the gal was he'd met with back there.

Younger was headed back to the street, looking for a cab when he approached him.

"Hey, Younger! I think you forgot something."

Younger swung around to see who was calling his name.

"Yeah, me. I think you forgot something."

"How do you know my name? Who are you?"

Theo pulled in closer, shoved a .22 into Younger's chest, grabbed his arm and pulled him to the side of the path.

"You're going to walk slow like with your best buddy, me, and we're going to have a little chat."

Younger paled and stood still, not moving. Theo pushed the gun a little harder into Younger's chest and they started walking. Perspiration beaded on Younger's forehead and he licked his lips.

"What's going on? I think you've made a mistake. I didn't forget anything. I don't know what you're talking about."

"Yeah, you did. A file folder you gave to that redhead back there. What was in it?"

Younger turned his head and looked back toward the Japanese Garden.

"Just a client I was giving some tax information she requested."

"She didn't look so happy. What you tell her, she owed Uncle Sam some big bucks?"

Younger's shoulders lowered, and he took a deep breath, "Yeah, that's what."

"What? Do you think I'm stupid or something? You flew up to deliver that? Why didn't you just mail it, huh?"

Younger pulled back, "How did you know I flew up?"

"I know a lot of stuff," Theo smirked.

Younger looked him straight in the eye, "Did you get a good look at her? Would you rather mail it or hand-deliver it?"

"Who is she, Younger, just in case I want to check your story out?"

"Why would you need to do that? Hey, what's with you anyway?" Younger said, trying to gain back some control.

"You and me, we're going to take a little walk."

Chapter Nineteen

Theo pushed Younger further into the park, along the Ninth Avenue entrance. To Theo's benefit there was no foot traffic on this side of the park that day and the shadows deepened the further in they walked. Younger's head kept swiveling, looking and hoping for some way out of this jam. But to any passerby, it would look like two fellas just having a conversation.

Theo laughed to himself. All he needed was information. But Younger didn't know that. He liked putting a little fear in his target.

Just as they came around the next set of trees, Younger tried to twist out of his grasp. Theo had a tight grip on the pistol and his finger caught in the trigger and bam! The gun went off.

Theo looked around to see if anyone heard the shot. Then he looked at Younger. Younger looked stunned as he slumped to the ground, a red stain spreading on his shirt.

"Damn!" Theo shouted. His assignment was to get information. This wouldn't go over so good with his boss.

Theo leaned down and checked the body.No doubt about it, Younger was dead.

Chapter Twenty

As soon as Bailey started reading the file, it felt like a dark cloud had fallen over that beautiful garden. She felt Younger's paranoia and glanced around to see if anyone in the park was showing any interest in her presence there. She got the usual stares, men trying to make eye contact when the women they were with weren't looking. *So predictable,* she thought.

This was too sensitive to peruse in the park. She needed to go somewhere more private and then question Peter about his "friend." She pushed the folder into her macramé bag and headed to the parking lot, leaving the serenity of the Japanese Garden behind.

Once Granger untangled himself from the school kid, he noticed that the girl was leaving the garden and decided to see what she was up to. Maybe she could lead him to wherever Younger went. He had to know what was in the file. His client would demand answers and since he couldn't follow Younger, it was the girl.

Bailey was almost to the Ford when she heard crunching gravel behind her. She turned quickly and almost knocked over a father and son carrying a kite.

"Sorry! Thought I dropped something." Bailey bent down to look at the ground.

"Do you need help to find it?" The man asked.

"No, thanks, I guess I was mistaken." Bailey smiled at them.

She put her hand in her bag and felt the comforting feel of her handgun. A.J. had insisted she get one and even helped her pick it out: a Walther PPK. It fit her hand perfectly, but she was warned that she had to be close in if she intended to use it. The gun fit perfectly in her bag and she had a license to carry it concealed.

For the first time since having the convertible, she felt exposed without the comfort of a top to protect and conceal her. Her hands were shaking as she tried to insert the key in the ignition. It took two tries. The old Ford started, she backed out of her spot. Granger reached her car just as she pulled out.

It seemed that the glamour and theory of being a PI had not prepared Bailey for the reality that this was a dangerous game she was playing. It was so simple when she was taking her investigative courses: she believed her pre-law courses had given her an edge, even though her grades weren't all that good - and then the stories A.J. had told her only deepened the mystique.

That's it, Bailey thought, *first call to A.J., second to Peter.*

Chapter Twenty-One

The old Ford was like a horse heading back to the barn, it seemed to drive itself over to Sausalito, and Bailey didn't remember the trip at all.

The weather inversion had reversed itself and the clouds were coming in early that February afternoon. It was only three o'clock but felt more like five-thirty. Normally, Bailey loved the seclusion of the fog wrapping around her garage apartment, but not so much today.

Today, she wished for bright sunshine like she had in Golden Gate Park, before her client gave her the file – the file she dropped in the bottom of her bag – the file that would decide what sort of future she had as a private investigator.

There was only one phone in the studio, mounted on the wall in the kitchen—inconvenient when she was asleep and the persistent ring woke her. The bruises on her shins attested to the lack of consciousness that accompanied her path to that phone. She kept saying she was going to ask the landlord if she could install another line, but funds wouldn't allow it right now.

She needed this case, any paying case, if she was going to make next month's rent. Her mother had been slipping small checks to her, but if her father ever found out, his roar would be heard all over San Francisco.

"Damn it, Veronica! She has to learn decisions have consequences."

And in that he was right, decisions did have consequences. Bailey couldn't put it off any longer. She picked up the receiver and dialed A. J.'s number, hoping he'd be near his phone. If he was doing surveillance, who knew when he'd be back.

"What?"- A.J. hated phones. He said they were an abomination because you couldn't see the expression in the person's eyes on the other side. He was a retired 20-year veteran of the San Francisco Police force. Never made lieutenant, never wanted to supervise – just do his job. And he did, closing case after case, until an injury to his right hand – he wouldn't say how – ended that.

A.J. – Bailey had asked one of the other investigators what the initials stood for once.

"Don't ever ask. I mean ever!" he cautioned.

A.J. answered the phone.

"A.J., it's Bailey. I need some advice."

"Of course you do."

"You still doing investigations for Gleason and McKinney?"

"Yeah, but things have been pretty slow over there, why?"

"When I interned over there, I had to sign a confidentiality agreement – standard form. Does that apply to investigators, too?"

"If you're doing a case for them, sure. Hey, what's this about?"

"Just got my first client."

"Congratulations, kid."

"A.J., I don't think congratulations are in order. Oh, to tell you the truth, I don't know what I was expecting – cheating spouse, runaway teen, collection of bad debt – not this mess that Peter put me in. This case is going to be much more complicated."

"Have you talked to Peter?"

"That's my next call."

"I take it Gleason & McKinney are somehow involved from your earlier comments, so I can't help you much. Boy, kid, when you step in it, you step in it. Can you walk away?"

"I'm so broke without this case, I'll have to panhandle or move into a commune, and somehow I don't think there's one for unemployed investigators."

"Just remember what you learned and break down the information. Keep good notes! Track who said what and when. Any inconsistencies, write it down and, kid, call Peter."

"Thanks, A.J. Thanks for listening to me grouse – and for not telling me, 'I told you so.'" Bailey hung up the phone.

She stared at the bag that held the file, took a deep breath and opened it, spreading the pages on the table.

The first pages were documents submitted by Gleason & McKinney on behalf of the client that was negotiating the merger; all the standard legalese and with attached accounting information outlining the deal's payout.

According to the documents, Hughes and Klein had been hired to audit the books to make sure all the accounts tallied – takeover company, Allen and Sons, and taken over company, Swift Investments. While doing this, apparently, Younger found some line items that didn't make sense.

There were asterisks next to the items he questioned. All of them concerned the investment accounts that were to transfer over. Younger's cover letter noted that he couldn't find any record of these companies even existing. Before calling it to his bosses' attention, he decided to talk to Peter and get an investigator. That is how Bailey got involved.

Deep breath, Bailey, she thought. *Get your facts in order before you make the phone call.* She wanted to wait until Peter was home and could talk freely. No need for someone overhearing the conversation.

The clock moved so-o-o-o slowly as Bailey waited. She knew Peter was putting in long hours at the law office preparing for his clerking with the federal judge this summer.

Chapter Twenty-Two

Bailey's father was a judge, and everybody called him "Judge." He always wanted a boy but got her instead. That didn't stop him from pushing her into what he thought was the only acceptable career: the law. Her mother, Veronica, thought the only acceptable career was to be the wife of an attorney. She ditched law school after interning at the law office, disappointing them both – no law degree, no husband.

The result was if she was going to "find herself," the Judge said she could do it without his financial support – thus the '52 Ford and the studio apartment in Sausalito.

Her tiny studio apartment was not conducive to pacing. There was barely room for her bed, a small table with one chair, and a kitchen so tiny it looked like it belonged in a kid's playhouse – the two-burner stove was crammed in so tight that she couldn't open the oven door and the cabinet drawers at the same time.

The bathroom – using the term loosely – was similar to those found in a travel trailer – a small corner sink with a toilet wedged in between it and the shower stall. That was one of the things she missed most about living at home – the large, soaking tub.

The most valuable part of the rental was that it was built over a garage where she could house her topless wonder – the Ford.

It was nearing five o'clock and Bailey's stomach was protesting the lack of food for the past several hours. She had been too excited to eat before the client meeting and too upset afterward.

She scavenged around in the cupboard until she found a piece of dried -out bread and the emergency peanut butter jar hidden behind the evaporated milk – how she ever thought that would replace milk – she could still remember the tinny flavor and decided it was best mixed in something like pumpkin pie.

It wasn't the five-course spread that she would have had at home, but no one could argue with the simplicity of the meal, and no clean-up as she dipped the dry bread into the jar.

Bailey thought about the first time she and Peter had met in the pre-law course on contracts.

He was slouched in the chair at the back of the classroom, doodling on his legal pad, his brown hair falling forward and covering his eyes. Observing him from that encounter no one would suspect that he had perfect recall. All he had to do was hear something once and he never forgot it. Good for classes, not so good for relationships.

She was struggling with keeping track of all the types of contracts that would be covered in the course and this guy's lackadaisical attitude was annoying the hell out of her. Apparently, it got to Professor Kane as well, because he glanced down at his seating chart and loudly called out:

"Mr. Peter Simmons, are we boring you?"

Peter glanced up and saw everyone staring at him.

"Excuse me?"

"Are we boring you, Mr. Simmons? Have a late night?"

"No, why would you ask that?"

"The other students seem to be paying attention and it appears that you are not so engaged."

Peter's eyes narrowed and he began to spew out all of the professor's lecture, verbatim, to the stunned professor and the rest of the class.

Bailey's first thought was: *This is someone I need as a study buddy!*

When the class was over, the other students gave Peter a wide berth, where Bailey made a beeline straight to him.

"How'd you do that?" She wanted to know.

At first, he stared at her without responding. She repeated the question.

"Don't know. It's just always been that way."

"Wow! I would love to be able to do that."

"No, you wouldn't. Trust me. You can never forget anything you see, hear or read. Makes arguments very redundant."

"Have you been assigned a study group yet? Could we partner up?"

"Why? I'm not a freak, you know." He grabbed up his books and shoved them inside his briefcase.

"Please. Look, I'm really struggling with these classes and if I don't pass, the Judge will make my life miserable."

"The Judge? What are you on probation or something?"

"What? No! That's what everyone calls my dad – The Judge – because, well, he's a judge. I'm supposed to intern this summer at a law firm and I'll never get the chance if I don't ace this class."

Peter reluctantly agreed and that forged a bond between them – he the "brainiac" and Bailey the fiery redhead with the big mouth.

Chapter Twenty-Three

Bailey called Peter at 7:30 pm. There was no way he'd be home any earlier than that.

The phone kept ringing. At this point, she wasn't certain if she wanted him to pick up or make her call back later. Then she heard the click.

"Hello?"

"Hey, Peter, it's Bailey."

"You know it's redundant to tell me your name, right? I know your voice."

"Right, right. Okay, that client you sent me? Carl Younger? Why did you recommend me? Did you know what it was about?"

"No, Bailey. Carl has always been a bit of a paranoiac, but he said that he was getting strange hang-ups when he worked late at the office ever since taking this assignment. He noticed the same car parked near his home that didn't belong to the neighbors. He just wanted someone out of Los Angeles to check things out. He needed someone to do a sensitive investigation, conducted by someone familiar with the law. It was a no-brainer: you needed your first client, he had the money to pay, and you had law experience. Why? Is there a problem? Did he hit on you or something?" Peter may have been attracted to his same sex, a secret that Bailey held close. Even in San Francisco, law offices and judges were not so liberal. but he was the big brother Bailey had never had and very protective.

"Nothing like that, no," she said, "It's just there may be a conflict of interest here. I can't say any more than that because of confidentiality, but that could exist on both sides of this case."

"Wow. It seemed like an innocent request. What are you going to do?"

"First, I had to know what you knew and when, and now I have to decide how to proceed. I definitely could use the money. By the way, what did you tell him my fees were? I have a cashier's check here for $500.00."

Peter chuckled, "Told him you were one of the most in-demand investigators and he'd better pay you top dollar if he wanted you to take the case."

"Well, thanks, I enjoyed it for a while, but the more I think about it, I know I can't accept this case. I'll have to return the money.

He didn't give me any contact information, said I had to call you if I wanted to get in touch. He told me the name of his accounting firm, but obviously, didn't want me to phone there if he told me to contact you."

"Are you sure, Bailey?"

"Peter, you know better than anyone about confidentiality issues – I can't do this, as much as it pains me to return the money."

"All right, then. I'll phone Carl in the morning and tell him that he'll need to find somebody else. I'll see who else I can recommend." Peter never reached Carl Younger.

Chapter Twenty-Four

Bailey leaned against the wall and hung up the phone. Giving that money back was going to be hard, but it had to be done. She wished she knew some way to get around the issue, but her dad had drilled into her rules about confidentiality and the law. If her taking this case was in conflict with her old law firm, then accepting the money was off the table.

It still nagged at her that Gleason & McKinney could knowingly be involved with something so underhanded. She had known Stan Gleason since she was a little girl. That's one of the reasons she got the internship. It certainly wasn't her grades. Her only "A" was in contracts and that was with Peter's help.

William McKinney, however, she didn't know as well. He had just joined the firm five years ago when it was clear that Stan's son,

Howard, had no intention of studying the law.

Howard had a passion for art and was studying in Florence, Italy with no intention of returning until after the Vietnam War had ended, to the dismay of his father who had proudly served in World War II.

Maybe the law firm didn't even know about the inconsistencies. Maybe they were innocent in all this. But, what did she really know about McKinney? Could he be doing this without the knowledge of Gleason? It just kept bothering her as she gathered up the pages and put them back in the folder. She had to find some place safe to store the documents until she could return them to Younger. If these got out, it could ruin the good reputation of Stan Gleason, and she couldn't let that happen.

Granger had followed Bailey to her place from Golden Gate Park. He'd caught up with her on the 101 and waited to see if she would go out again.

Suddenly he was startled by a sharp knock on the car window. There stood a very irate woman asking what he was doing parked outside and staring at her house.

"You'd better move along or I'm calling the cops! I got your license, mister!"

Granger believed her. Even though her speech was laced with a heavy Italian accent, he understood every word she said. At least he had information to give his client. He knew that Carl Younger had made it to San Francisco and who he'd met with. The bad news was he didn't know where Younger was now.

He reluctantly called his client and told him what happened. That didn't go over well. Allen read him the riot act and then said he'd check and see if anyone had seen Younger back in LA. He was informed to stay where he was and track the girl.

She was their only lead at this time, and he didn't know her name.

Chapter Twenty-Five

Bailey glanced around the tiny studio, looking for any place that she would consider safe enough, when there was a knock on the door.

She called out, "Who is it?" while looking for someplace to stash the file, finally secreting it under the mattress, then grabbing it out again, knowing that was the first place somebody would look.

"Bailey? Hey, it's me. I saw your light on and thought I'd check to see if you'd eaten anything tonight."

"Just a minute!" She turned, saw the freezer and shoved the file inside.

With a sigh, Bailey opened the door to her landlady, Sophia Romano. Bailey got this apartment because she helped Sophia out of a jam by finding a loophole in the town ordinance about building apartments over garages: saved Sophia a big fine and got Bailey a place to live.

Sophia felt it was her "duty" to take care of Bailey as long as she paid her rent on time - her generosity only went so far.

Sophia sniffed the air. "Peanut butter? Again?"

"How do you do that? I've never met anyone who has such an acute sense of smell!"

"My family's vineyard. You learn to use your nose to tell you when to harvest, when to transfer the wine into the casks, and when to bottle. It's nothing special," she shrugged.

Sophia plopped herself down on the only chair, leaving Bailey to hastily push the covers aside on her unmade bed. This wasn't a quick "dinner" check. There was something on Sophia's mind.

"Well, little one, what have you gotten yourself into?" Even though Sophia was barely five feet tall, she always called Bailey "little one."

"Huh?"

"Earlier this evening, I see this man. He is parked in a car across the street in front of the grassy strip and he is staring up at your place."

"What makes you think I did something?" Bailey glances over at the freezer.

"How long you lived here?"

Bailey thought. "Let's see about six months. Yes, exactly six months."

"And how many men have you had over here, not including that nice, young man, Peter."

"Not many."

"NO ONE! And now this man, he's staring at your place? I thought that was your job, staring at people? Isn't that what a private investigator does?"

Bailey smoothed the covers on the bed with her left hand as the questions ping-ponged around her brain. How could someone have found her so soon? Maybe there was someone tailing her at the park. Maybe she wasn't just being paranoid.

"So, Sophia, is this 'mystery man' still out there?"

"No, he left when I went out and asked him why he was staring at your window."

Chapter Twenty-Six

"Oh my God, Sophia! What if he had been dangerous? Had a gun or something?"

"No, I scared him good. Told him I was going to call the police and that I had his license number," she chuckled. "You should have seen that car move!" She repositioned herself in the chair.

"This chair, not so comfortable."

"Well, thanks Sophia, but please, don't do anything like that again. Just call me or call the police. Please, promise me?"

"Just because I'm old doesn't mean I can't take care of myself! I handled those Fascists just fine in my country." She pushed down on her knees and rose from the chair.

"Mange, little one! You are getting too thin. No more peanut butter. Real food!" she said as she moved toward the door.

"Yes, Sophia, no more peanut butter." Bailey closed the door behind her. She heard Sophia's footsteps as she made her way down the stairs.

Now what? she thought. Sophia was right about one thing. She was supposed to be the one watching. What a rookie mistake! Not checking to see if she was followed! Like she could blend in with an old green car and her flaming red hair blowing in the wind.

When she applied for her gun license Bailey thought it was just a precaution, not that she would ever need it. Now, she felt for the presence of the gun in her purse and moved it to the bedside table.

She had decided to not pursue this investigation, but whoever had tailed her, didn't know that. The circumstances made the information in that file even more important. There must be some truth to it or why the interest in her? Someone at the park must have seen Carl give her that file.

There were only two windows in her place: a tiny one in the bathroom, that even a cat would have trouble climbing the mossy siding in a completely vertical plane, and the one in the front that looked over the Bay, where that grassy strip separated the road from the water.

She closed the curtains and peeked out through the side, looking for a car, any car. It was quiet, but Bailey knew she wouldn't sleep tonight. She wouldn't sleep until she could get rid of that cursed file. It was probably melting the ice cubes right now, it was so hot.

She slid the chair into the corner between the bed and the window, placed her feet on the bed and proceeded to stake out her own place. Her eyes were getting heavy, so she brewed a pot of strong coffee. She hated the bitter taste but had learned to tolerate it when she was in college. Before that she had been a tea drinker, but that was considered to "prim and proper" for her roommates, hence her evolvement into coffee drinking.

Bailey could still smell the burned coffee that had permeated her college dorm room, where there was always a thick brew heating on the "forbidden" hot plate. Soon, she was as addicted to it as the rest of the students cramming for tests into the wee hours.

Chapter Twenty-Seven

Bailey's head knocked against the side of the window and she realized she had fallen asleep. She jerked up and looked at the clock. Six-thirty. Damn! How long had she been out?

Pulling the curtain back a little further, the light was just started to signal daybreak, and the road was clear – no strange cars parked anywhere. Maybe, Sophia's aggressive stance had scared the "looker" off. Probably not for long, Bailey thought. The sun weakly shone through the fog that surrounded the Sausalito Bay. Sophia was sweeping the walkway, turning her head from side to side, straining to see around the gnarled Monterey Cypress that partially blocked her view of the curve in the street. The sounds of her humming floated up on the still air.

Bailey dropped the curtain back, took a sip of the strong coffee and started re-reading the file that Carl Younger had given her the day before. Really? Could it only be a day ago that all this started? She looked in the scrap of mirror over the bathroom sink and felt like the morning after one of those proverbial cramming sessions.

She pulled a comb through her tangled hair, used her lipstick for eye shadow, blush, and then finally put it on her lips. Her beauty routine was basic and cheap.

Her first goal was to see if she could have any luck tracking down those investment companies. That meant City Records and she had a contact there.

Chapter Twenty-Eight

Granger decided to return to Sausalito to be closer to the girl, but not so close to get rousted by that little Italian woman again. She was like a mama bear protecting her cub.

He smoked a cigarette, never cared what brand, just whatever was available, inside the motel room he'd booked for the night. He flipped through the yellow pages, trying to locate an all-night photo place so he could get his film developed. His best bet was back in San Francisco so he headed back across the bridge.

The photo shop Granger chose was in the seedier part of North Beach, but the price was right and the prints would be ready in about three hours. In the meantime, Granger walked the streets and mulled over the day's events. He still couldn't figure out how Younger got out of his sight so quickly. He smoked another cigarette, leaned against the side of a building that promised the "sexiest women in Frisco" That term was only to lure the tourists. San Franciscans hated that term; he declined the "great" offer to go inside. The huckster didn't hassle him. He knew how to shift and sort his clientele. Granger didn't worry about declining the offer as many servicemen and others took advantage.

As promised the photos were ready and he headed back across the bridge to his motel.

Back in his room, he flipped through the pictures, discarding the "fake" tourist shots, keeping the ones focused on the girl. He held up the picture that showed her full face. She was striking, that's for sure. The kind any guy would go for, but he needed to find out how she fit into the whole Younger thing.

Chapter Twenty-Nine

Next morning Granger woke up early and grabbed a cup of hot coffee in a paper to-go cup from the diner next door to his motel. It was muddy and hot, just the way he liked it. He drove over to Humboldt Street where he had tailed the girl yesterday. Now that he knew the layout, he positioned himself around the bend in the street and waited, smoking another cigarette and drinking his coffee.

It wasn't long before he saw her car drive by, heading in the direction of Highway 101. He followed two cars behind and kept to the speed limit. She stopped at a small grocery on the edge of the highway. He waited on the shoulder of the road. She came out a few minutes later holding some kind of plant – plants weren't his thing and he was totally confused.

She parked downtown near the City Municipal building. Granger guessed she was checking something in that file Younger gave her, but he needed to see exactly where she went. He parked three spaces behind her and followed her inside the building. He stopped to look at the list of offices, looked down at a scrap of paper in his hand and nodded his head, like he had found where he needed to go.

Granger used his peripheral vision to track her progress. She didn't pause anywhere on her way through the building. It looked like she knew just where she was going.

She stopped at the end of the hall where records were kept, tried the door knob, but it didn't open. She glanced at her watch then leaned against the door.

Granger doubled back and turned right at the next corridor. She'd have to pass by his post when she exited. Figured he had enough time to use the facilities. When he exited he found a chair with an ashtray next to it by one of the doors in the hallway. He sat down, lit a cigarette and prepared to wait.

A woman with screaming red hair came out of the ladies' room and headed down the corridor.

After about ten minutes, Granger made his way back down the hallway toward the records office. When he opened the door, there was the same woman, with the reddest hair he had seen on anyone since "I Love Lucy."

"Excuse me. I thought I saw an old classmate of mine come in here a few minutes ago. Is she still here?"

"Do you mean, Bailey? She's down in the stacks."

"Oh, no, guess not. My friend's name is Anna. Sorry, I only saw her from the back. It's been a while. I guess my memory is not as good as I thought. You have yourself a nice day."

Now he had a first name. He didn't have to keep referring to her as "the girl." He left the building and headed back to his car to wait. There was a sidewalk stand on the same side of the block, so he picked up a cup of coffee and settled in.

He had two things to report to his client when he checked in this evening: her name was Bailey and she was doing something in the City Records office.

Chapter Thirty

One of the duties of a law clerk is foraging through piles of city and county documents for the law firm's clients' cases. No way would one of the partners be caught dead spending hours in the dusty tombs of legal documents filed in the City Recorder's office; Bailey had spent hours there and learned that the quickest way to get to the files she needed, was to befriend the assistant clerk, Tiffany Rogers.

Tiffany did not resemble her name at all. When asked about her name Tiffany told the story that her mother had been obsessed with the Tiffany store she saw in an ad at the hairdressers and thought that was a name that would ensure her daughter would escape the trailer-park living where she was born. Her mother was thrilled when she moved to San

Francisco, sure that her name choice was what did it.

Tiffany's passion was her cat, Homer. She kept a picture of him on her desk and he was so large that he dwarfed the chair he was photographed on. Orange with white stripes, he possessed a smug look as he stared into the camera.

Tiffany's eating habits were the bane of the offices, particularly her fondness for boiled eggs and the accompanying repercussions of that indulgence. Bailey's way into the office was to inquire about Homer and bring some sort of treat for him. Food offerings to Tiffany were suspect and treated with insulting disregard.

It had been a year since Bailey had been into the City Recorder's office, not that she was sad about that, but she had to stop and pick up a catnip plant for Homer before making her way to the building.

The files were stored in the lower bowels of the city building. Dust, mildew and mice were rampant. Maybe that's why Tiffany liked her cat so much. Bailey always made sure to take plenty of tissues down there with her.

The problem was, she wasn't sure what she was looking for. Incorporation papers? Security filings? She thought it would be better to start checking with the years prior to William McKinney joining the firm and then through to the current ones, just in case her mistrust of McKinney was warranted.

All these filings were public record, so she would be able to access them. She just wasn't sure what "story" to tell Tiffany about *why* she needed them.

Bailey was waiting outside the Recorder's office when Tiffany arrived in the morning, holding the catnip plant with an orange bow tied around it.

"Oh, by God! Where have you been? Someone said you left the law firm and became a private investigator, but I told them they were nuts! Oh, Bailey, that is the cutest thing! Homer will love it!" Tiffany always talked in exclamation points.

Bailey stared at Tiffany's hair. It was bright red. "Your hair?"

Tiffany patted it and posed, "I know, isn't it wonderful! I got the idea from you and just insisted that my hairdresser match that picture I took of you!"

Bailey snapped her mouth shut and mutely nodded her head, "Wow," was all she could manage to say.

Once she got her wits about her, she wondered if she should allow Tiffany to continue to think she was still with the law firm, but then decided that at least a little truth would be the best. She didn't want to burn the only entry she had into city government. Besides, Bailey seemed to remember that Tiffany's cousin was a police officer somewhere and she didn't want anything said at the family dinner.

"Well, the rumors are true. I did pass my classes and got my PI license. Mostly boring stuff so far; not much different from all that research I had to do for the law firm. In fact, that's why I'm here. Have to do some legal research for a client. I guess it's the same old, same old."

"Well, you just tell me what you need, and we'll get you started."

Bailey gave Tiffany the list of filings she had compiled prior to coming down. She knew it wouldn't be easy, but sometimes the answers were in the most mundane of paperwork. She'd seen it time and again researching law cases.

Chapter Thirty-One

Granger had just inserted his last nickel in the parking meter when she came out and headed back to her car. He sat up quickly, started the car and looked around for traffic coming beside him. He saw a break and pulled out, managing to get a break in the traffic right ahead of her. Sometimes it was better to tail a car from the front, but he wouldn't have done it if he hadn't seen how beat and dusty she looked. He figured she was headed back home.

It was easy to track her drive back to Sausalito, even in the commuter traffic; that red hair glowed like a beacon in the setting sun. He was sure he wasn't the only one following her progress that late afternoon.

Sure enough she took the exit that would get her down to Humboldt Street and eased down behind the curve where the big Monterey Cypress blocked him from view.

Chapter Thirty-Two

Bailey had gotten a description of the car that had been parked out front from Sophia the other night. Her powers of observation were not so bad that she'd miss a certain gray sedan showing up wherever she was going. Never too close, but always nearby. She couldn't get a clear look at the driver, but she was sure it was the same car.

She sighed; *maybe it's just my paranoia kicking in.* Peter told her that Carl thought he was being followed, but, no, she had that prickly feeling on the back of her neck that was her personal sign that something wasn't quite right. She reached up and rubbed the area under her hair.

What neither Granger nor Bailey knew was there was someone watching both of them. Someone who could have answered all their questions, but as the saying goes: then he'd have to kill them.

Chapter Thirty-Three

Bailey had showered the dust off and had just turned on the radio. When the phone call from Peter came.

"Hello," Bailey hummed into the phone receiver.

"Bailey, its Peter."

"You know it's redundant to tell me your name, right? I know your voice."

"Touché."

"Hey, did you get a hold of Carl?"

"That's why I'm calling. There's no answer at his apartment and I made a quick call to his firm, you know, friend to friend, and they hadn't heard from him either. In fact, they didn't even know he was in San Francisco. I checked the airlines, but there were only two going to LA that afternoon and there was no record of him making either of them."

"Geez! There was someone parked outside my place yesterday after I got back from the meeting with Carl. My landlady, Sophia scared him off, but what if something happened to Carl. How do we track him?"

"You're the Private Investigator, what do you think we should do? I can't spend a lot of time on this, I know he's my friend and all, but this is your bailiwick, not mine."

"You're right. Sorry. Guess I'm still new to all this. Let me think this through. I'll check the hospitals and see if there are any reports of injured men of his description being brought in in the last day. Maybe he was mugged coming out of the park or something."

"Good idea. Look, I hate to leave you like this but there's a case going to trial tomorrow and I have to make sure all the "t's" are crossed and "i's" dotted."

"Right, right, I was talking out loud, remember that's an old habit of mine."

"Drove me nuts when we were in study group."

"I'll phone you tomorrow and let you know what I find out."

"Bailey, do I need to tell you to be careful? Right now, we have more questions than answers and I don't want to dial *your* number and get no answer."

"Trust me; I'll be looking over my shoulder the whole way."

Bailey hung up the phone, made the hospital calls and no luck.

After releasing her sore fingers from the holes in the dial and stretching out her kinked back, she closed the book and knew the next call was to the police.

Problem was, she was an outsider, a private investigator without police experience. She didn't have any friends on the force and nothing to trade for information. A catnip plant wouldn't do the trick. The only person she really knew who had contacts was A.J. and she wasn't sure if she should play that card right now. How was she ever going to earn her creds if she didn't figure this out herself, and soon?

How could she check Central Police Station without knowing who to call? She paced the room and gnawed on her fingertips.

Think, Bailey, *think!*

Then it hit her! Tiffany's cousin. But wait. She had never contacted Tiffany outside of office hours before. She didn't even know if she had her home phone number. She could always try the phone book. Had to try.

Back to the phone book, Bailey scrolled down the list of Rogers listed there and couldn't see a Tiffany, but hey! There was a *Homer* Rogers. That couldn't be a mistake. With all the crazies out there, no woman wanted to list her name in the phone book anymore.

Smart cookie, Tiffany, thought Bailey.

Okay, now how to get the contact information from Tiffany about her cousin, Bailey couldn't even remember his name, if she ever knew it to begin with.

Tiffany would be home from work now, it was after six, so Bailey took a deep breath and dialed the number, hoping she had solved at least this *small* mystery. The phone started ringing and she tapped her toe in rhythm to the tone.

Finally, someone picked up.

"Hello."

"Tiffany? It's Bailey."

"Bailey? How did you get this number?"

"The phone book."

"But, I'm not listed."

"Ah, you forget! I'm a private investigator now," Bailey laughed, "Sorry, it was your cat's name that gave it away."

Chapter Thirty-Four

"So, much for being clever," Tiffany said, "Did you forget something in the stacks?"

"No, no, I was just talking to a friend and mentioned that I knew someone who had a cousin on the force. That was you right?"

"Yes, my cousin on my father's side, Melvin Rogers."

"Right, right, now I remember, he works out of the Central, right? What's he up to these days?" Bailey was praying that he was in homicide or a detective or something useful.

"He's still at Central, right, working missing person cases."

Bingo!

"Well, how about that!" Now, Bailey was speaking in exclamation marks.

Okay, now came the tricky part. Bailey had to figure out how to make contact with

Melvin without giving anything away. Always lead with a bit of the truth: interrogation 101.

"Gee, that's really weird, because my friend I was telling you about, was concerned about a friend of his that didn't show up for an appointment, and like, this guy *never* misses an appointment. Do you think I could call up your cousin and see what he thinks?"

"That should be alright, but why doesn't your friend contact the police himself? I mean, it's his friend and all."

Bailey felt like she was on a high-wire without a net. "*What a tangled web we weave, when first we practice to deceive…*" was running through her head, but she had to come up with something fast.

"The thing is, he just had to leave tonight for, hmm, Portland, and he won't be back for a week or so and thought maybe I could do him this favor and I said, 'Sure.' You know how it is, right?"

There was silence on the other end of the phone and Bailey felt she had messed this up big time.

"What? Oh, sorry, I was just filling Homer's dish. It should be no problem calling Melvin. You know he's still single? Things didn't work out with his last girl. She left to join the Peace Corps, and he's been looking to get back in the swing of things. Hey, why don't I call him, and you could have coffee or something?"

"Ah, sure, I mean once I get this other thing handled." Bailey had to leave the door open, even though she wasn't sure she was ever going to walk through it.

"Well," Tiffany said, "I'll call him and give him your number. It's the one on the card you gave me this morning, right?"

"Right. Thanks so much, Tiffany, I really, really appreciate this. Hope Homer enjoys his gift. See you again soon, bye now."

Whew! Bailey did a little dance around the room. *See, I can make my own contacts. Hah!*

Chapter Thirty-Five

Well, nothing was going to happen with finding Carl tonight. Bailey decided to make her obligatory phone call home. She already had a hand cramp from all the phone calls she had been making.

Dialing the number, she thought, maybe she could wrangle a dinner invitation. It was only a little before seven and the Judge never ate before seven-thirty. She had been on a roll, so maybe this one would pan out as well. She wasn't looking forward to spending the night propped up in the window again.

"Hello. Stephens residence."

"Good evening, Marge, it's Bailey. Are my parents home?"

"Well, goodness gracious, haven't heard your voice for a while."

"Yes, been so busy." They both knew but wouldn't admit the real reason Bailey hadn't been around. The last time, she had come to show them her brand new PI license and you would have thought there was a 7.2 earthquake the way the dishes rattled from the Judge's bellow.

It was a good thing that there were no near neighbors, or the cops would have been called.

If Bailey had thought he'd be proud of her, she was very much mistaken. He accused her of making a fool of him and what kind of game did she think she was playing.

"Private investigators are cop wannabees and losers who couldn't make it on the force," he roared.

"Judge, you use private investigators all the time, every law firm does."

She should have stopped then. Whenever he was daunted, in any way, he'd go for the jugular and this was a moment he wasn't going to let pass, and then she made the mistake of trying to enlist her mother's help.

"Mother, you've always said to do what makes me happy, well, this makes me happy."

"Judge, I tried it your way, but that's not me. I'm an adult now. It's time I made my own decisions."

"You know what? You're right. That's it! Now, you're dragging your mother into this discussion? You've always done whatever you wanted, no matter what advice we have given you. Pack your things and move out! If you want to make poor choices, you won't do it under my roof."

Bailey shook with the memory of that confrontation: her mother's tears, her father's pacing, and Marge staying out of harm's way in the kitchen. It'd been six months since she'd been to the house. She hoped that things had cooled down, but she never knew with the Judge.

"So, Marge, are they home? How is the Judge this evening?"

"Bailey, your mother's here, but the Judge is at a committee meeting. I made pork roast for dinner and was going to serve it in about 30 minutes." Code for, the coast is clear come on over.

"That sounds yummy. I'm on my way."

Chapter Thirty-Six

Bailey changed into a skirt and clean shirt, grabbed her keys off of the hook, reached down to turn off the radio as she headed for the door. She had her hand on the radio knob when the phone started ringing.

"Damn!" She decided to let the answering machine pick it up. That had been her biggest expenditure when she became a PI. She hesitated and waited to see who was calling.

"Bailey, its Peter. Are you there? Pick up its important."

She ran back to the kitchen, banged her shin on the table and grabbed for the phone.

"Peter, I'm here!" She punched the stop button on the recorder and sat down on the side of the bed. "I've checked all the hospitals and no one matching Carl's description has been brought in. I have a possible contact in the police department. I should know something tomorrow."

"Bailey, stop. I have something to tell you. The police just contacted me. It's about Carl."

She heard Otis Redding's "Dock of the Bay" come on the radio as she looked out the window at the swells of the ferries, the phone in her hand.

"Bailey, Carl never made his flight."

"Oh, did he stay over?"

"Carl's body was found floating in the water at an old pier caught in a fishing net below Pier 39."

Bailey sat on the side of her bed and heard a buzzing sound in her ears. "Bailey? Bailey? Are you there? Did you hear what I said?"

"What? Yes, I heard you. I just don't understand. How do you know it was Carl? Why, did they call you?"

"Apparently, he had identification on him. It was water-logged, but readable. My business card was jammed inside the side pocket of his wallet. The police wanted to know if I thought Carl was suicidal or could give them any reason he would be down by the Pier."

"Oh, Peter! Did you tell them about me?" Bailey asked in a panic.

"Hey, give me some sense. Of course, I didn't say anything, but I'm not going to impede an investigation. As an attorney, you know I can't, but I'm not going to make you a sacrificial lamb either. After all, I'm the one that got you into this mess."

Bailey leaned back against the pillows that made her "headboard" against the wall, closed her eyes and shivered.

"Peter, I don't know what to do! I'm in way over my head. This is my first case and, believe me, I never thought I'd be in a mess like this. If I turn over the file Carl gave me, I could be causing a lot of trouble for Stan, and if I do that, the Judge is going to hang me as well. Which reminds me, I was supposed to be going over there for dinner when you called."

"You were invited to dinner? That's progress."

"No, the Judge is at a committee meeting and I was going to talk my way into a pork roast dinner. I knew my mother wouldn't turn me away, if I just showed up. Better call Marge and tell I'm not coming."

"No. Go. I don't want you there by yourself tonight. You already said that someone had been watching your place. There's nothing we can do tonight anyway. Please, Bailey, go."

"Alright, I have to tell you I'm not too happy to be sitting here all night either. That was one of the reasons I called the house in the first place."

"I'll be done here about ten. How about I hang out at your place tonight? Then, we'll decide what to do tomorrow morning. That work for you?"

"Sure you're not going to mind sleeping in a chair?"

"Just give me a blanket and the floor and I'll be fine."

"Peter thanks so much. I'm leaving now. I'll phone you when I get to my parents' house and again when I'm headed home."

"Keep an eye on your rear-view mirror and do those evasive driving techniques you learned at your PI school."

Bailey laughed as she held down the receiver hook and then called and told Marge that she was running a little late, but that she'd be there soon.

Bailey checked that the file was well hidden under the ice trays in the freezer. That cashier's check kept calling her name.

She grabbed a scarf off the coat stand by the door, wrapped it around her hair and added a warm jacket before grabbing the keys. She turned on the light outside her door and turned off the overhead light but left the table lamp on in her apartment before she locked the door behind her. No way she was coming home to a dark place *this* night.

Chapter Thirty-Seven

Bailey removed her gun from her bag before lifting the garage door. Everything was quiet and still. The fog had drifted in and it was hard to see very far in front of her. This is when Bailey really wished she had a top on her Ford. Maybe she'd see about getting it replaced once she started making some money. It wasn't too advantageous to be so exposed in her line of work.

She checked the backseat before getting in, put her gun in her oversized pocket and then started the car and backed out. Some water dripped down her back as she passed under the raised garage door. It sent a chill down to her bones.

Was Carl dead when he was put in the water? She wondered, then turned up the collar on her coat, retrieved her gun as she got out to lower the door back down, checking the woods around the place.

Bailey was thinking that A.J. had been right. Being a private investigator was a lot less glamorous than it showed on television shows and in books. Her courses for her license were mostly memorization and with her law background, that part was easy. She guessed since so many in her class had military or police experience, there was no need to point out the scarier parts of the profession.

Chapter Thirty-Eight

Bailey noticed a familiar gray sedan following her when she got onto Highway 101 heading toward San Francisco. She caught a glimpse of it when it passed under a street lamp just as she hit the on ramp.

There was no way she was going to lead whoever was tailing her to her parents' home. Even though it would have been easy enough to find out *where* they lived, whoever was following her didn't need to know that's where she was headed.

It was after seven in the evening, so she didn't have the cover of commuter traffic that was all going the opposite direction. She decided to try a little diversion when she entered the lane for the toll plaza. She stopped and told the toll taker that she was being followed and gave him the description of the gray Mercury. It was three cars back and in the same lane as she was.

"He's an old boyfriend and he just won't take 'no' for an answer. Is there anything you can do to help me? He really scares me. He used to be a boxer." Bailey's eyes welled up with tears.

The toll taker looked at the car she indicated. "Not to worry," he smiled at her, "I'll think of something." "Oh! Thank you so much! He really is an awful person. My father warned me about guys like that. I should have listened."

The cars behind her were honking for her to move along, so Bailey moved past the toll plaza and eased her car into the far-left lane, so she could see the toll plaza in her side mirror. When the gray Mercury pulled up to the toll booth, the driver was shoving a bill at the toll collector. He took the bill, held it up to the light, pretended to check a list on his clipboard. He directed the other cars around to the other lanes and told the driver to wait right there. The toll taker leaned in and said something to the driver. The barrier pole remained down. Bailey's car pulled further and further away and then vanished in the fog covering the Golden Gate Bridge.

She turned on the radio. There came Otis's mellow tones singing about his "Dock of the Bay." Bailey whistled sadly along with him: the most iconic part of the song, which was actually used to cover up the fact that Otis didn't have any lyrics for that portion of the melody yet. He died before he could re-record the song.

Chapter Thirty-Nine

Bailey reached her parents' house without a tail. The house always gave her a thrill whenever she saw it. The red bricks and arched multi-paned windows were glowing with lamp light. The house had been in the family since the Gold Rush era. The Judge liked to brag that it was built so well that not one brick moved during the 1906 earthquake.

Her favorite room was the library where the Judge had his carved wooden desk that had come around the Horn on a sailing ship. The Judge wasn't the first judge in the family. When they came West during the Gold Rush, it was to a lawless region that needed lawyers and judges and the Stephens had just the mettle to deal with those "ruffians," as the Judge liked to call them.

The room was lined with bookshelves in a warm oak with alcoves containing photographs of past generations standing in front of the house. The trees were bigger, and the clothes had changed, but the stern look of the Stephens men was reflected in the portrait that the Judge had commissioned when he was appointed to the bench.

Her father had attended the University of San Francisco Law School, the same one he had insisted she attend, if she wanted him to pay for it anyway. The Judge mistrusted those lawyers with fancy East Coast degrees, saying they only got it because of *who* they know, not *what* they know. Somehow, he didn't see the irony in that as all of the West Coast Stephens had gotten into law school that exact same way.

Bailey pulled the car around back and parked in the open space behind the Reynolds place; they always spent the winter in Tahiti. This way if the Judge came home early, she could make an easy getaway.

She still had a copy of the key to the back gate, so she let herself in and walked through the miniature maze garden that one of the previous family members had had put in after visiting England. Bailey had always thought it was pretentious, but then her taste was to simpler plantings.

Bailey knocked on the window of the kitchen door and smiled as Marge turned, wiping her hands on the apron she always wore. Marge hurried across the floor to let her in, then gave her a big welcoming hug.

"I have missed you!"

"Well, if the Judge would just come around, I'd use the front door. I still have my key. Any softening in that area?"

"Now, Bailey, you know he wouldn't discuss anything like that with me."

"How's your grandson doing, Marge?" She said as she moved into a hug.

"We've got so many eyes on him he can't move without somebody reporting it!"

Marge actually knew exactly what was going on in that house, but her loyalty to the Judge would not allow her to say a word against him, Bailey knew. She wasn't clear on all the facts, but the Judge had intervened when Marge's grandson was acting up and got some charges thrown out. The biggest defiance she would participate in was letting Bailey return home on the "QT." Marge had practically raised Bailey, while her mother attended numerous committee meetings and social events while serving as the Judge's representative. It didn't allow a lot of time for a precocious child, like Bailey.

The kitchen was filled with the scent of roasted pork loin and Bailey could see the simmering pots with all the side dishes on the stovetop.

"I guess I'm in time then? Oh, Marge, I have really missed your cooking! Did you tell my mother I was coming?" she asked anxiously.

"Don't worry, she's looking forward to seeing you. I think the Judge knows she sees you on the sly and secretly hopes you'll repent and stop all this private investigation nonsense."

Bailey had been seriously considering that on the ride over, but just hearing that about the Judge, made her dig her heels in even further. There was no way, she was going to admit she was wrong, even if it killed her—which with everything that had happened over the past day, could be a distinct possibility. She guessed she got her stubbornness from the Judge.

"Marge, I have to make a quick call. I'm supposed to meet up with Peter later, okay?"

"Of course."

Bailey dialed Peter's number, got his answering machine and left a message that she was at her parents' house and would phone when she was headed out. Bailey removed her jacket, hung it on a hook by the door, smoothed her skirt, and pushed through the door that connected to the dining room and made her way into the room on the opposite side. It was a pretty room. If the library was the Judge's domain, this room was her mother, Veronica's.

Done in various shades of lavender and trimmed in white, the sofas were comfortable enough to sit on, but not so much that it was difficult to rise. Decorum meant a lot to her mother. Bailey knew her mother loved her, it's just that she didn't fit the ideal of a frilly, girly, acquiesced girl that she envisioned.

"Hello, Mother."

Veronica's hair was gleaming in the lamplight. It was white now but had been as red as Bailey's when she was younger.

"Bailey, it's good to see you home," she said in her soft voice. The Judge's voice shook the room and her mother's whispered; perfect counterpoint to each other.

They walked arm-in-arm back through to the dining room, her mother taking her normal spot at the end and Bailey sitting to her right. It seemed so comfortable, it was hard to believe that this was the first time she had sat at that table since the "confrontation." After that, Bailey would meet her mother at a tea room her mother favored. She would have loved to confide in her mother, but she knew that she was incapable of understanding Bailey's decision. Hers was a different era, as they agreed to each take their own path.

The dinner Marge prepared was delicious, but Bailey had a hard time eating. She couldn't help but think this wouldn't be the best advertisement for her fledging career, her first client getting murdered and all. Not that it did Carl Younger any good either.

"Bailey, what's going on? Something's on your mind, do you want to talk about it?"

"Mother, really, everything is fine," she patted her mother's hand, "The food is delicious, thanks for letting me stop by."

"Is it money? Can I give you a check to help out?"

"Oh, please, Mother, it's nothing like that, truly, I just wanted to see you and make sure everything was okay at home. I can always find someone to tell me about the Judge, but I just needed to see *you* tonight and tell you I love you."

"Bailey, what is all this?" Her mother pushed her chair back from the table. "Now what's going on? You're scaring me. It's this investigating thing, isn't it?"

"Mother, calm down, everything is fine, really. I guess I was just a little homesick. Sorry, I didn't mean to upset you. Really, I'm okay. Things couldn't be better. I received my first fee from a client. I'm good." She wasn't going to tell her that the client was now dead.

Veronica sat back down, took a sip from her wine glass, rubbed her forehead and sighed. "I know the Judge has been tough on you, but he really worries about you. Ever since you were a little girl, you were always pushing the envelope. You had to go the highest on the swing, climb the tallest tree, ride your bike faster down the hills. The scrapes and cuts; we cornered the market on iodine and Band-Aids. I think, secretly, the Judge was a bit proud of all your exploits. He was so proud when you entered law school and so disappointed when you dropped out."

"But, Mother, sitting in that office, day after day, was killing my soul. We come from a long line of adventurers, it's just in my blood, and surely, he understands that?"

"Maybe deep inside."

"Look, I hate to eat and run, but Peter is dropping by tonight. I'm helping him with some research on a case that goes to trial tomorrow."

"Oh, how is Peter? I always liked him."

"He's a great friend, I'm glad I have him."

"Friend?"

"Yes, Mother, *friend*."

Bailey rose from the table, kissed her mother's cheek and promised to call again soon. When she went back into the kitchen, Marge had packaged up food for her to take home.

"Marge, thanks but you didn't have to, I'm eating."

"Oh, I know. Peanut butter, right?"

Bailey hugged her and carried her goodies out to the car. She made sure to check her surroundings and the back seat before getting in. She had laid an old blanket across the seats to keep the fog's mist from dampening them, climbed in and started the motor. That old Ford may have not been much to look at, but the motor worked just fine.

It was a good thing the alley behind the house was one-way, because just as she began to turn right onto the street, she saw the Judge's Cadillac pulling in at the other end.

Chapter Forty

Bailey thought she saw that same gray sedan she had lost at the toll booth parked further up the street. She slowed down when she went passed but didn't see anyone inside. Bailey had barely gotten home when Peter knocked on the door and announced himself. She flung the door open, gave him a quick hug and pulled him in after her.

"I don't know if I'm being paranoid or not, but I passed a gray sedan parked on the street when I was coming home. It's possible I'm being followed." Bailey peeked out between the closed curtains.

"Peter! What are we going to do about all this? Is there any way we can keep these files confidential until we know more of what happened to Carl?"

"Actually, yes, he was your client and he did pay you, so what was discussed between the two of you is considered confidential under California State law. The same as if he had hired you as his attorney. The good news is you can keep the money. The bad news is, you're working for a dead man and your assignment has changed. It's up to you to do what you can to solve Carl's murder, not protect your old law firm, so there may come a time to pass that file over to the police."

Bailey knew he was right. He usually was. So, there it was: she was a professional private investigator. This is what she had signed up for and this was the reality of the situation. She knew from her training that she couldn't impede an official police investigation, but she had to find out exactly what the police knew.

"Who are you supposed to see tomorrow? I know you have that court case, so when are you going down there?"

"Detective Kwok. He works out of the Central Station. It was assigned to him because of the body's location. God! Listen to me! It's not a body, it's Carl. Damn it anyway." Peter pulled his fingers through his hair.

"I'm so sorry, Peter," Bailey leaned over and gave him a hug and smoothed his hair back from his face. "We'll figure this out. So what time are you going tomorrow?"

"I called the law firm and told them what happened, so they let me give all my notes to second chair. It'll be good experience for her and I told her I'd be down to the courthouse as soon as we finished."

"Okay, listen, Peter, don't sleep on the floor. It could be hazardous to your health, in more ways than one. I could trip over you, and you could get a sore back, so we'll just share the bed, no harm, no foul."

Peter's preference for male companionship made it an easy offer.

"I'm too spent to argue. Thanks, Bailey, I think we both needed each other tonight."

Bailey smiled and fixed the covers on the bed. When they were settled, she turned off the light and through pure exhaustion fell deep asleep.

Granger had left his car back at the bend in the road and had moved to a better viewing area standing under the trees. He saw a man go up to Bailey's place and the quick hug, some moving around and lights out.

Who was this guy? Granger wondered and what is his connection.

"Did you really expect a girl who looks like that to not have someone?" Granger muttered to himself. He stamped out his cigarette and headed back to the car.

Chapter Forty-One

The next morning, Bailey made a pot of coffee while she scoured around for something to make for breakfast; Peter didn't consider dinner leftovers appropriate breakfast fare; Peter's choices for breakfast were not as prosaic as hers. Just as she turned away from the refrigerator, Peter handed her some money.

"I'll keep lookout until you get back. Then I'll hop in the shower."

Bailey gave him a hug. "I'll pay you back you know."

Bailey eased her car out of the garage looking for any sight of the "reappearing" gray sedan. Her head was on swivel as she drove down to the corner store, grabbed a dozen eggs, bread and orange juice.

Peter was notorious for long showers, it was the one thing every roommate of his had complained about – even with the drought - so Bailey had a semblance of a proper breakfast by the time Peter was done in the shower. He'd brought his clothes in a garment bag. He hated wrinkles and was always dressed impeccably when appearing in court, down to the shine on his shoes.

Bailey and Peter drove into San Francisco in separate cars. Bailey was following Peter and keeping an eye out for that gray sedan she had seen following her the night before.

Sophia was too brave by far, and Bailey didn't know how dangerous this stalker was. If she continued to see that same car, she'd have to figure out a way to draw him out.

They approached the city in a slow procession. It was Thursday. They had left a little after nine to avoid as much traffic as they could going across the Golden Gate Bridge.

Peter exited and Bailey was right behind him. They both pulled into the parking garage across from the station at the same time.

After last night's debacle at the toll plaza, Granger had taken his rental back and picked up his tan Oldsmobile Starfire sedan from long-term parking. He made sure he was far enough behind Bailey's car to not be picked out. He had to hand it to her; it was a pretty good delaying tactic. She had a quick mind, he liked that.

It took him a while to figure out what she'd done. He still remembered his confusion when the toll taker wouldn't take his money right away.

The guy held it up to the light like it was phony or something, then checked a list on his clipboard, before leaning toward his car window.

"Hey, buddy. You've got to learn that when a girl says, no, its no."

"What?"

"Your girlfriend just told me that you've been pestering her. Leave it be, buddy."

"I don't know what you are talking about." he'd said, but by the time he got the toll paid, Bailey's car was nowhere in sight.

This morning, Granger was keeping Bailey's car in sight, he exited into the wharf area, not far behind her. Granger didn't want to park anywhere where he had to pay to get out, so he pulled into a curbside space just as another driver left. He watched as Bailey and the guy from last night, crossed the street and went into the station. Maybe her boyfriend was a detective? Naw, he was dressed too well for that. More waiting, but he was going to be more alert this time.

Chapter Forty-Two

"Good morning, my name is Peter Simmons and I have an appointment with a Detective Kwok."

The sergeant on duty checked his roster and told Peter to have a seat and he'd let the detective know he was there. Peter and Bailey sat down on the hard, scarred bench and watched as he placed the call.

Bailey's stomach flipped all over the place and she felt like that "proper" breakfast was going to do a repeat showing.

"Peter, how are you going to explain me being with you? What if he wants to talk to you alone?"

"If that's the case, just wait here, but he just wants to touch base and see what I can tell him about Carl. I told him on the phone that he was a buddy from college and I'd help any way I could. I'm a lawyer remember, I do this for a living. I'll answer all the questions he asks truthfully and only the questions he asks, okay? If he asks something that directly involves you, I'll have to tell him. We are not going to be accused of obstructing an investigation, understood?"

Bailey did. She was a judge's daughter and at this point she didn't care much about protecting Stan Gleason, Carl Younger was dead, and Bailey wasn't sure she could find out why any easier than the police could. Maybe, she should just turn everything over. But part of her was just stubborn enough to want to hang on. What kind of PI was she going to be? Even following a cheating husband could be dangerous as one of her instructors recounted in class. The cheater's wife came after him with a knife when he placed the pictures proving her husband's infidelity on the kitchen table. He said to make sure you present damning evidence in a place with no visible weapons.

The best piece of advice Bailey received came from a woman PI who had been doing the job for about five years. She carried a six-inch blackjack tucked into the back of her trousers and a low-cut blouse for distraction. She learned that after getting a horrific beating while following an embezzling employee. She was no match for his fists and spent two weeks in the hospital and six months recovering. Bailey would have thought she would have quit after that, but it just made her more determined to not let it happen again. A year of jujitsu and practice with the blackjack made her someone to be reckoned with. You didn't want to meet her in a back alley. Bailey had practiced her moves with that blackjack until she could do it in one smooth motion.

This was Bailey's trial by fire and she decided right then that she would cooperate with the police, even turn over the file if necessary, but if she couldn't find out *who* did this to Carl, she'd find out *why*.

They hadn't been sitting there very long when a detective checked in with the desk sergeant and was pointed in their direction.

"Good morning, I'm Detective Kwok."

"Peter Simmons. We spoke on the phone last night about my friend, Carl Younger."

"Yes. I'm sorry about your friend. Could you come back and answer some questions?"

"Of course, but I do have to be in court shortly."

"I'll make it quick." He glanced in Bailey's direction, "And you are?"

"A friend of mine, Bailey Stephens," Peter said.

Detective Kwok nodded and asked her to wait there, pushed open a high gate on the right and ushered Peter back.

Chapter Forty-Three

Bailey sat back down on the bench. She didn't know if she was relieved or not. She would sure like to know what they were going to talk about, but with Peter's recall, she knew she'd hear it word for word.

She decided to use her time reviewing the list that A.J. told her to compile. When she wrote things down, they cohered for her, all the random thoughts and pieces of information would form a more complete picture. Bailey always carried a notebook inside her bag.

Bailey used that method in college and repeatedly at the law offices. She had the knack of finding the connection between supposedly unrelated facts. Peter's recall and her ability for combining tidbits made them a dynamic duo in class.

She took it out and drew a circle in the middle of the page with Carl Younger's name written inside, with arrows pointing to different people: Peter, her, Gleason & McKinney, Hughes & Klein, Allan & Sons, and Swift Investments, a question mark for her mystery stalker. From those names, she added additional arrows pointed to possible relationships that she didn't know yet. Those were the only contacts that she was privy to in this investigation.

When she went to the records office, she found the filings for several of the companies Carl had on his list, but none for the ones he had put asterisks next to; namely, Dixon Industries, Almeida Smelting, and Bancroft Industries. She couldn't find them on any stock market exchange and wondered the same thing Carl had: why are they on the list?

Something about those companies had led to Carl's death. She was sure this wasn't some mugging gone wrong. So, she added those names, too.

Granger saw a phone booth at the corner. Maybe it was time for a report to see what his client wanted him to do and see if Carl Younger had shown up. He dialed the operator and gave her the number. She told him how many coins to deposit and when the clanging sounds signaled he had deposited enough, his call was connected.

"Allen and Sons, how may I direct your call."

"Granger Williams calling for Michael Allen."

"One moment while I connect you."

"Well? What have you found out?" were Michael Allen's first words.

"First, here is the number I am calling from. I don't have a lot of coins, so I need you to call me back."

"Sure, what's the number?"

"415-555-9898. I'll be here. I'm tailing the girl, so I have to make it quick."

Granger hung up the phone and told the guy waiting outside the booth that he would be awhile and maybe he should look for another phone. Just as he finished with the disgruntled wannabe caller, the phone rang.

He nodded at the guy as if to say, "See?"

"Hello, Granger."

"Okay, what's going on?"

"First, has Carl Younger shown up there?"

"No, as of this morning, his firm still hasn't heard from him and there's no answer at his apartment. I even sent someone around to check and his neighbors said he hasn't been home since Tuesday."

"When I took this case, it was a simple follow and report. Is there something you're hiding? Because that girl I'm tailing just went into the Central Police Station here in San Francisco. I think she picked up that I was tailing her and if I'm blown, I might as well come back and see if I can locate Younger in Los Angeles. Maybe he rented a car and drove back."

"Hold on a sec, I have another call coming in."

Granger lit a cigarette and tapped his toe, keeping an eye on the doors into the police station. He'd have time to get to his car, because Bailey would take time exiting that garage. But he was prepared to hang up the phone if need be.

"Granger?"

"Yep, I'm here. Now, I was saying..."

"Hold it. That was Dan Hughes, from Hughes and Klein, the auditors that Carl Younger works for, or should I say *worked* for. He just got off the phone with a Detective Kwok, from homicide in San Francisco. Younger's body was pulled from the water near Pier 39 yesterday."

"Shit! What happened, did he say?"

"It appears he was shot and then dumped in the Bay. This changes everything. I had my suspicions about this company we were merging with and that's why I suggested Hughes and Klein do the audit, but Younger kept delaying the report."

"Do you want me to come back or continue surveillance on the girl? Her name is Bailey by the way."

"First name or last name?" Allen asked.

"Don't know for sure."

"Have you figured out what her connection is to Younger? Could she be in danger? Or have something to do with his disappearance?"

"Don't know the answer to that either."

"Stay up there another day. I think the best approach would be to keep an eye on the girl, Bailey, and I'll see what I can find out on this end."

"Those are all good questions and ideas. I don't have the answers right now, except, he did give her a file, that much I know. Right now, she's at the police station with some guy. I'm thinking it's got something to do with Younger. I have a buddy who was in the MP's with me. I heard he was on the force here in Frisco. Let me see if I can learn something from those channels and I'll call again tomorrow."

"Do it. I don't know who we're dealing with, but this is a lot deadlier that we thought. Watch your back. If you saw Carl give this girl something, maybe the killer did to."

Granger let that sink in, hung up the phone, lit another cigarette and moved back toward his car. What if by tailing Bailey, he was bringing the killer right to her? He thought about the guy he'd seen her with this morning. He didn't look like the kind that could protect her if she got into trouble.

He pulled out his address book from the glove box and started looking through the names. So many had multiple crossed out addresses and others written above or beside or under the entries; he'd told himself, repeatedly, to start a fresh one, but he kind of liked looking at where everyone had been and where they were now.

Jim "Mac" Mackey's number was one of those that showed his progression from discharge to his hometown in Virginia and then out here to Frisco; LA natives, loved seeing the cringe from Bay area people when someone said "Frisco." Going home had not been the homecoming he had envisioned; his dad was still a drunk and his mother had taken a hike right after Mac went in the service and he could no longer protect her from his father's abuse. He'd met a girl in California when he was stationed at the Presidio and found his way back to San Francisco. The relationship didn't last, but he'd found a home in the police force and had been here about five years now.

They always meant to meet up, Los Angeles and San Francisco were not that far apart, but they just hadn't made it happen. Granger felt bad that their first contact would be to get information, but Mac was pretty easy going; it was probably that Southern way of doing things.

Chapter Forty-Four

Bailey was gnawing on the end of her pencil when she felt a tap on her shoulder, her head jerked up and there was Peter. She gathered all her papers together, shoved them in her bag and followed him out of the station.

She had a hundred questions, but as they hadn't called her back to be interviewed, she assumed that Peter hadn't mentioned her name.

"So far so good," Peter answered without her asking. "The detective wanted background and asked if Carl contacted me while he was in San Francisco. I told him that I didn't even know he *was* in town, and I didn't until you called me and asked me to contact him for you."

"I don't feel good about this."

"Bailey, do you have a dollar?"

"Ah, sure, do you need it for something?"

"Just give it to me. "

Bailey reached into her purse and handed him a dollar.

"As of now, you are my client. Everything we talk about is privileged and every conversation we've had in the last two days is confidential as well."

Bailey nodded her head. Of course! She forgot that he had passed the bar this last September. "Thank you, Peter. I'm hoping your services won't be needed, but it's nice to know I'm covered, nonetheless. And I'd say your rates are reasonable," she added.

Peter chuckled.

"Did they give you any information about what happened to Carl?"

"No, he was pretty tight on the details, but that's to be expected in an ongoing investigation. He just mentioned he had been shot once in the chest and then dumped in the bay."

"It's a wonder he was ever found."

"I think that's what the killer was counting on. Look I have to get to court, so I'll call you this evening. I have to go back to the office to prepare for tomorrow's session. It might run late."

"That's fine. I've got to go over these notes and check in with A.J. Hey, Peter, you're sure I can cash that check?" Bailey had taken it out of the freezer earlier.

"I want you to. It's the closest thing to a contract you have with Carl. We need to give you whatever protection we have until we can figure this thing out."

She gave him a hug before they headed back toward the parking garage.

Granger didn't know which precinct Mac called home, but he did have a number and decided to go back to the phone booth and try it when he saw Bailey and Peter walk out of the station.

Chapter Forty-Five

Bailey left Peter at his car, drove out of the garage and headed over to the nearest Bank of America to deposit Carl's check. Her account had not seen that amount of money in a long time. She could actually pay her rent, buy some groceries and put more gas in her car; she was just sorry it came with sad baggage. But she was determined to earn every penny of it.

On her drive back to Sausalito, she pondered the next steps in her investigation. It was imperative that she find information on those three companies that Carl had been checking on.

She needed to talk to A.J. The last time they talked on the phone, she wasn't able to reveal much of what was going on, but the situation had definitely changed.

Granger pulled in a few cars behind Bailey's Ford as she exited the parking garage.

It was easier for him to blend in with the traffic, nothing flashy like in the movies – those guys wouldn't last two days on a stakeout without being spotted. But then again, he wasn't doing too good lately, that's why he was thankful for the traffic. He'd been spotted twice now. Granger was glad he had picked up his Olds Starfire from the airport.

There were cars everywhere and the congestion was a help and a hindrance, as he dodged pedestrians and cable cars. He was stopped at a light, when she pulled into a space in front of a bank.

He turned right and idled on the side street until he could see where she went. Then made a U-turn heading back the way he'd come. He circled around the block. Luckily there were no traffic lights on the side streets and he could cut through the alleys behind the businesses to not waste time.

Just as he reached the corner, she was getting in her car and pulling out of her parking space and into traffic. Tailing her was getting tougher as the traffic increased.

He was far enough back but could see her entering the ramp for North 101 and felt comfortable enough to suspect she was headed home.

Chapter Forty-Six

Granger had to figure out if he should contact her, for her own protection, of course, nothing else. Whatever was going on, it had reached a critical stage and he didn't want her to be dodging him all the time. *He* wasn't the enemy, but then again, he didn't know how innocent she was in all this. Maybe she had set Younger up. He needed to learn more about who "Bailey" was. Why was she at the police station today? And who is that guy she's been with? What's his role in all this or is it totally unconnected?

Since he didn't have any resources in San Francisco, he had to give Mac a call and arrange to meet up with him. He needed to know what he could tell him about Younger's murder.

Granger was a few car lengths behind Bailey's open-topped Ford. He knew better than to get too close after the incident at the toll plaza. His training had him looking at the other cars on the road. He noticed one in particular. A burgundy Chrysler. It wasn't making any attempt to blend in. When Bailey changed lanes, it changed lanes. Granger moved in a little closer to get a look at the driver. He saw a swarthy man who didn't take his eyes off the car in front of him – Bailey's car.

He tightened his following, moving to the lane on the right of the other driver, that way he could block his exit if he wasn't just an innocent driver anxious to get home after a rough day's work. Granger was surprised that Bailey seemed to not notice him. Whatever she heard in that police station had certainly affected her.

Chapter Forty-Seven

There was no doubt now. The car was trying to merge over into the right lane when he saw Bailey's turn signal. Granger stepped on the gas and came up on the right side, blocking his exit. Theo had to slam on the brakes to not sideswipe Granger's car. Then pulled in tight behind Granger and mouthed some appropriately foul words while giving him the middle finger salute. Granger just shrugged at him and mouthed, "Sorry."

During this maneuver, Granger was able to get a better look at the driver. His eyes were close together and his bulk was barely contained by his suit. Definitely not someone you would look forward meeting in a dark alley. So, what was his connection to Bailey and why was he intent on tailing her?

In order not to give away his connection to Bailey, Granger turned off at the next right turn. He thought he knew where Bailey was going, and he made a quick left that put him on a parallel street as the exit lane. He gunned it and came out ahead of Bailey, driving past her place. She wasn't there. He was puzzled and was about to turn around thinking maybe that brute had gotten to her after all, when he ducked down and watched to see if the car following Bailey went past or parked nearby. He didn't know that Theo already knew where she lived. The man's burgundy Chrysler crept by and then turned at the next corner.

Just then Granger saw her pull in, take some groceries out of the car. He had parked in a driveway that from his previous stakeouts he knew the owners were gone until after 7 pm. She was safe, for now.

Chapter Forty-Eight

When Bailey left the police station, she wasn't sure where she was headed. The ramifications of her dilemma with the police, what to tell them and what not to, seemed to deepen with every mile as she headed across the bridge back home. If she'd been more aware, she would have noticed the car following her – make that two cars. She had picked up another interested party.

Bailey felt like she was a "damsel in distress" on the ride home from the police station. If she panicked every time there was a hiccup in a case, then her father was right, she wasn't cut out for being a private detective. What were the first things she had done? Phoned A.J. and Peter. It was time for her to get herself together or this would be her first case and her last one, if word got out.

Bailey had stopped by the corner market, picked up some much needed items, including another jar of peanut butter, and headed to her apartment. She put the car in the garage, unloaded the groceries, then went downstairs and knocked on Sophia's back door. Sophia always said that back doors were used by family and friends, front doors were for strangers.

There was no answer so Bailey pushed the envelope with the rent money - Sophia only wanted cash, she said cash didn't bounce - between the screen and the door, wedged in the doorsill. She was sorry Sophia wasn't home. She could have used her no-nonsense words, plus her kitchen was always fragrant with garlic, oregano and basil. Bailey would always ask Sophia how to make her fabulous sauce and the answer was always the same:

"Old family recipe, you'd have to marry into the family to get it. There is my cousin's boy, he's single," she would say. There seemed to always be a cousin, nephew or family friend available in the Romano clan.

She turned and walked toward her place when she smelled cigarette smoke. It could be from anywhere, but she never recalled having smelled it around her place before. Sophia didn't smoke and neither did she. Bailey's hair on her neck stood up.

Chapter Forty-Nine

Bailey climbed the stairs and when she got to the landing, she stopped like she was looking out over the bay, pushed her hair back and opened the door.

Too many things had been happening too fast. She knew she had been followed and spied on, but suddenly the cozy, safe apartment seemed anything but.

She locked the door behind her and realized that she needed a deadbolt on the door. Bailey would talk to Sophia about having one installed even if Bailey had to pay for it. It was all these precautions that she was going to have to put into place if she was going to continue this career path.

Bailey put the rest of the groceries in the cabinets and dialed A.J.'s number. She pulled her notes from her bag and made herself a sandwich, one-handed, while she waited for him to pick up. She had just taken a bite when he answered.

"What!"

For a minute all Bailey got to do was mumble into the phone's receiver.

"Who is this? I don't have time for jokes. Speak up or I'm hanging up this phone!"

"Sorry, A.J., it's Bailey, I had a mouthful of sandwich and the bread glued my mouth shut."

"That's what you get for eating that white bread, no substance."

They had had this conversation before. A.J. was a firm believer that the only bread a San Franciscan should eat was sourdough; it was hardy and made even a homemade sandwich taste like it came right from the deli.

"Right, right, look can we not talk about my choice of sandwich slices right now? I need your expertise, big time. You remember the case I told you about the other night?"

"Yeah, some confidentiality concerns. How did that work out?"

"Not so good. My client's dead."

"'Not so good' is an understatement. How did he die? How did you find out?"

"Peter called me. The police found his card in the guy's wallet and called him. I don't know what exactly happened, but Peter was told he was shot and dumped in the bay. He washed up near Pier 39, that's all I know."

"Have you talked to the cops yet?"

"No, Peter did. He was able to keep me out of it for now. I wouldn't know what to tell them anyway. I don't know if this is a mugging and it might not have anything to do with that file I told you about. Maybe he was just in the wrong place at the wrong time."

"Sure, you keep telling yourself that, kiddo, and you're gonna end up the same way. Look, no fooling around now, I'm coming over there and we'll brainstorm this thing. This is too heavy a load for a newbie like you."

"I'm so relieved. A.J., I feel like I'm in quicksand and there's no branch in sight to grab hold of."

"I'm on my way. Still at that place on Humboldt?"

"I have some leftovers from home I can heat up for us," Bailey offered.

"If Marge cooked it, it'll be worth eating. I'll bring the bread." He couldn't help his little dig, but Bailey didn't care. At that point, the cavalry was on its way and it couldn't get there fast enough for her liking.

The fog was fingering its way across the bay and getting caught in the trees and what was left of the sun was disappearing over the hills when A.J. finally arrived.

Bailey shared her diagram with A.J. After talking things over, they agreed to reassess the situation after Detective Kwok got back with Peter.

There wasn't much they could do that night. A.J.'s parting words were, "Keep that gun close, Bailey."

Chapter Fifty

As Granger waited there, he realized that it was time to introduce himself to Bailey and see if they could figure this situation out. He didn't want to leave her alone tonight. He didn't know what that thug wanted with her and at this point, didn't even know how she fit into his case. It was time to call his client.

An old dented Chevy pulled into the driveway. An older man climbed the stairs, knocked once.

"Hey, it's me," the man said.

Bailey let him in. Granger thought he looked like someone who could handle himself.

Granger figured Bailey would probably be safe with someone there. He backed out and headed back to his motel, stopping at a convenience store to top off his gas, pick up more cigarettes, and get change for the phone.

Granger went into the coffee shop next door and ordered the meat loaf special. When he was finished, he asked for some coffee to go, bought another pack of cigarettes from the vending machine by the door. His motto: *you see them, you buy them*, and returned to his room.

He pulled out the contact information for his old buddy Mac, dialed the motel operator and asked her to connect him. She told him she would get him an outside line and the charges would be billed to his room.

He waited for the tone and dialed Mac's number. He didn't know his schedule, so hoped he had an answering machine, more people were getting them. He figured since he was a cop that might be mandatory. He stubbed out his cigarette in the ashtray and waited for someone or something to pick up.

"This is Jim Mackey; please leave a number, the time you called and a return number after the beep and I'll get back to you as soon as I can."

Well at least it was a good contact number. Granger hadn't been sure what with all the scratch outs and everything. He waited for the obligatory "beep."

"Hey, Mac, it's a voice from your past, Granger Williams. I'm doing a job up here in your neck of the woods and thought we could catch up. I'm staying in a motel here in Sausalito; the number is 415-555-2345. I'm in room 223. Hope to talk to you soon."

Granger lit up another cigarette and pulled out his notebook. He flipped back to the beginning and read back his notations. He took a drag on his cigarette as he waited for Mac to return his call.

Chapter Fifty-One

Bailey watched the clock waiting to hear something from Peter about Carl. She kept drawing circles trying to tie up loose ends but kept coming up short. There was so much she didn't know.

Peter finally phoned Bailey around five. Detective Kwok had called him with the details of what had happened to his friend. Carl had been shot at close range prior to being dumped in the bay.

Apparently, Carl's body had been caught by a discarded fishing net and brought in by the current. Bad luck for the killer, good luck for the detective. The body had not been in the water long enough to disguise the time of death, which was shortly after he had left his meeting with Bailey. Not good news for Bailey, though. How could she establish her innocence? Only the man and his son who talked to her on the way out to her car, and it was obvious she wasn't carrying a 200+ pound body on her back for dumping in the bay.

What Bailey couldn't know at the time was there was another witness: Granger.

When Bailey hung up the phone, she collapsed into the chair next to her bed. Not good, she said to herself and went into the kitchen, headed for her comfort food: peanut butter. She stood at the window looking out over the bay toward San Francisco as she dipped her spoon into the newly -opened jar.

Had the killer seen her talking to Carl? Was that who was following her? Was there more than one? Bailey almost bit through the spoon when those thoughts came into her head.

Then she froze. Most important, did this person see Carl hand her the file? It was time to give A.J. an update call. None of her private investigator classes handled being stalked by a killer. It was a little after six in the evening when Bailey dialed A.J.'s number. He said his caseload was pretty light at the moment and he always ate dinner between 5 and 6, so he should answer the phone. It rang a couple of times and Bailey heard his customary greeting, if you could call it that:

"Yeah?"

"Hey, A.J., it's Bailey."

"Had a feeling you'd be calling about now. Heard a dead body showed up. Could it be that client you were talking about?"

"Have you been tapping my phone or something?"

A.J. laughed, "Nah, just heard that a body turned up in the bay with a bullet hole in his chest and somehow I immediately thought about you."

"Somehow that doesn't reassure me."

"Hey, you were the one who said they found your client dead. I wouldn't be much of a detective if I didn't figure out the one they pulled out of the bay was the same one you told me about."

"Okay, A.J., just checking in like I said I would," Bailey said. "I want to figure this out myself, but to be truthful, I think I'm being followed. I didn't tell you last night, but I smelled cigarette smoke when I climbed the stairs."

"Hey, you know if you need me to come back over there I will, right?"

"Thanks, A.J."

"I'm serious. It'd be my butt if the Judge found out I let someone whack you on your first case."

Bailey sighed as she hung up the phone then straightened her shoulders ready to put her plan in action.

It was time to put all her research together and find out who killed Carl. She was going to treat it like the research projects she had done at the law firm – yes, she hated to admit it – but she guessed the time she had spent there would actually pay off. Wouldn't that just cause the Judge to puff out his chest?

Anytime the attorneys were preparing a case to go to trial, they laid out a timeline and where anyone who could have been involved was located. They did a background check on each one who stood to gain from the crime, and what their movements were before, during and after the incident. From what she had seen it was not so different than how the police put their case together – but often working from opposite sides of the evidence.

Since Peter's law expertise was corporate law, she knew that when she ran into a "sticky" spot where she needed clarification, she could ask – not for advice, but in the form of "research." Same had to go for A. J.

There was nothing like the space for the whiteboard and conference tables to spread documents on like at the law firm, so it was time to get creative. She found her stash of brown paper bags under the kitchen sink and started ripping them along the seams to form large pieces of paper. She dug through her junk drawer for masking tape and began taping the pieces together to form one large piece and taped it to the wall behind the door. She didn't want someone coming in and seeing it – especially Sophia. There would be too many questions to answer. And, quite frankly, she didn't have all the answers. To know those, you had to know the questions. And those were what she was about to write down.

She dug through her old briefcase, found a black marker and a yellow highlighter, and tested them to see if they still worked, made a fresh pot of coffee, and closed the drapes for privacy.

Chapter Fifty-Two

Ever since Younger's death, Theo knew he had to cover his tracks with his employer. Sabana was not someone you ever wanted to cross. No one he knew of had. Word was no one *alive* had.

Not only did he not have the file, he had killed the only person who knew where it was. He had searched Younger's briefcase and body, but he only found his airline ticket and receipt from the taxi – standard "accountant" stuff and a phone number scribbled in a small notebook, the kind reporters and cops used. Theo had stashed Younger's body in some shrubs, near an unlit parking space. He waited until dark to load Younger's body into the trunk of his car, glad the Chrysler Imperial had a big trunk, and then drove over to the docks. Theo honed his dastardly trade in

Brooklyn where a body dumped into the sea would be carried away to some unconnected location – away from the scene of the crime. Dumping the body in the Bay seemed logical, but since he wasn't supposed to be dumping a body, Theo didn't know about the tides in the Bay and had miscalculated big time. The body was found a lot sooner than he expected so he had to come up with a plan.

The only person Younger had contact with in that park was the redhead. He had Younger's notebook. Maybe he could find her that way. Theo flipped through the pages. Everything was dated and timed – what an anal ass – Theo thought. Younger's precise note-taking was going to lead him right to the girl. Theo smirked.

It took him a couple of times ringing all the recent numbers before someone finally picked up. Even though he had never heard the redhead's voice, he imagined that's how she sounded. Hmm, now just find out her address and the rest would be easy.

The only problem was he couldn't use his normal contacts to trace the phone number to an address. There was no way he was going to alert his boss about this "hiccup" in getting those papers. Then he remembered his old buddy, Mario, who could find anybody. He had set up shop in the North Beach section of San Francisco – topless bars and seedy offices. Theo smiled. He would enjoy the trip.

Mario's office was upstairs in the middle of the block on Vallejo Street. Mario teased Theo about him calling it "Valley Jo." What did he know about Spanish pronunciations? And he didn't much care. Right now, he needed information, not a language lesson.

"Yeah, yeah, I gave you the phone number, what you got for me? I need that address. Were you able to do it or not?"

"Wow, we haven't seen each other in five years and no, 'Hello, Mario, howse ya doing?'"

Theo stared at him.

"Okay, what's the rush? No time for a slice of pie? They've got great pizza down the street. Not as good as Brooklyn, but there's enough Italians to not make me too homesick."

Theo didn't say a word. Mario sighed, "Not a social call. Look, I wouldn't put up with this attitude of yours if I didn't owe ya." Theo had gotten him out of a rough spot with one of the neighborhood toughs in Brooklyn back when they were kids.

He slid a piece of paper over his desk to Theo. "Maybe sometime you'll tell me what this is all about." He looked at Theo's deadpan face and added, "Then again maybe not."

Theo picked up the piece of paper, glanced at the address, started to leave the office, then turned around and asked, "So how do I get to this place?"

Heading out of town over the Golden Gate Bridge, Theo had to figure out a plan. It had to be perfect. No more screw-ups. He found Bailey's place about two in the afternoon. There was a front house and a place over the garage. He'd have to figure out which one was hers. He parked across the street on the water side and lit a cigarette. It was quiet, didn't look like anybody was home.

Suddenly, a little woman, looked like his Aunt Floreen in New York, flung open the door, glared at him and started toward him with a broom. Now, Theo had been on the receiving end of brooms in his life and stared at her. He threw his cigarette out the window, started the car and pealed out of there before she could get off that porch and over to his car. He could see her shaking the broom at him from his rear-view mirror.

Such a tough guy, Theo, he muttered to himself as he sped down the street.

Theo came back in the morning. Saw the redhead come down the stairs with some guy. Theo smiled as he saw her get into the green Ford convertible.

That was two days ago and she didn't even catch on he was tailing her.

Chapter Fifty-Three

Bailey thought of herself as a "damsel in distress" and that was also how Granger saw her. He'd seen a lot of capable women in the military, but everything about Bailey brought out his protective side. And he had information she didn't. He knew someone was following her and it seemed to him that it hadn't even crossed her mind. But, he now knew that he wasn't the only one watching the shadow against the light in Bailey's apartment. Somewhere in the trees was the other one – the one that Granger knew was dangerous. He'd seen too many like him in his line of work and pretty wouldn't count for squat against him.

Granger saw the determined set of Bailey's jaw when the porch light caught her as she came up the stairs after slipping an envelope into the old lady's door. It had replaced the "deer in the headlights" look she had had coming out of the police station. He wasn't sure what had changed, but it could make her too complacent.

She hadn't left her apartment all day and if Granger was going to convince her that she needed his help, he was going to have to do some background on her and quick. The hairs on the back of his neck – his danger indicator – were warning him that they were running out of time.

Chapter Fifty-Four

Theo was tired of waiting to get that file and knew he couldn't dodge his boss any longer. It'd been three days and he kept getting squeezed out. No matter what the risk, he had to move and he had to move tonight. Failure wasn't an option. He knew Bailey had the papers, she had to, and if she didn't he had ways of making her tell him. He smiled when he thought of some of the ways he could convince her. Theo was getting that file tonight.

Theo crushed out his cigarette under his heel and crept through the trees and brush that surrounded the apartment above the garage. He waited until the lights went off in the main house – the Italian lady might have been old, but she was a little too bold for him to mess with right now. He was focused.

There were pine needles under his feet which caused a muted crisp sound and emitted a sweet scent of cedar.

Theo could see Bailey moving around in the apartment as a shadow behind the curtains. It was a frantic movement, movement in space and with her arms. He had no idea what was going on, but it didn't matter. This was it.

Theo was so focused on that window, that he didn't sense that someone had come up behind him until he felt pressure on his neck and before he could make a sound or see anyone, everything went black.

Granger had been ready to leave when he noticed the movement on the other side of the woods. The guy was so mesmerized by the window, that he never even heard him come up from behind. His military training kicked in and it was just like being back in 'Nam.

The big guy dropped like a stone and now Granger had to figure out what to do with him and how to secure him before he came to. He checked his pulse to make sure he was still breathing – it had been awhile since he'd used that technique. Satisfied that he was out, but alive, Granger had to find something to secure him with before the brute woke up.

He moved over to the garage where Bailey's car was parked and carefully raised the garage door and looked around on the shelves to see if there was any extra rope or twine that he could use. Just as he was reaching for the oily rope that was on a hook in the back of the garage, he heard the sound of a gun being cocked and a throaty voice said, "Hold it right there."

Bailey stood holding the gun in the stance she had been taught during her training and said, "Drop the rope and turn around."

Granger couldn't believe that he had gotten the drop on the bruiser following Bailey and had been stopped in his tracks by Bailey: first she spots him tailing her and now this. His only excuse, he told himself, was she was savvier than he thought.

He turned around, thought of throwing the rope at her, but decided that it was time that they met face to face and to tell her that they were on the same side. The gun was wavering in her hand, so the chance of getting accidentally shot was too high to confront, so he dropped the rope, took a breath and said, "I think you're going to want me to use that rope on that man that's been stalking you," and motioned his head in the direction of his downed opponent.

Bailey quickly glanced over to her right and saw a man prone on the ground underneath the old cedar tree. She moved her head back to the man she was holding her gun on, took a breath and then asked, "Who are you and how do I know you're not the dangerous one?

I saw you tailing me on the bridge the other day."

Granger wanted to rub his head, which he often did when he was trying to figure out how to explain something but didn't dare move.

"Right. Well, I was trying to find out what happened to this guy I was following for a client. But this guy on the ground, he is definitely someone you do not want to mess with. That move I used on him won't last for much longer, so how about I lower my arms, tie him up and then we can have a reasonable conversation about this situation."

Chapter Fifty-Five

Bailey looked at the man on the ground and saw that he was starting to twitch and knew she didn't want to deal with him. The guy looked too strong and too bullish for her tastes. She decided to trust her instincts and ask for help.

"Okay. Slowly move over and take that rope and tie him up, but I'm warning you, any move in my direction, I will shoot first and ask questions later. Understood?"

Granger lowered his arms, stooped down and picked up the rope where it was lying at his feet. He backed away with his eyes on Bailey until he was next to her stalker. He hog-tied Theo and then sat back on his knees and waited for permission to get up."

She nodded, kept the gun pointed at him and motioned him to go over to Sophia's back door. She pounded on the door with her foot until a light clicked on in the kitchen and Sophia came to the door and yelled "Who's there?"

Bailey said, "It's me. I need some help with a situation here."

Sophia slowly opened the door, peeked around the corner, saw that it was indeed Bailey and opened it more fully with her baseball bat in hand.

"What you doing waking me up like this? And why you got a gun?" Sophia raised her bat higher.

"I found this man in my garage and another one is tied up under the tree. I need somewhere to sort this out and your kitchen is bigger than my whole apartment."

"Okay, okay. Do I need to get my gun?"

"You've got a gun, too?"

"Of course!"

Bailey looked at the man in front of her and shook her head, no, then said, "Maybe later."

She walked him into Sophia's kitchen, warm from her stove, and sat him at the scarred oak table in the middle of the room.

Sophia lowered her baseball bat, told Bailey she would be right back and stalked out of the kitchen. Soon she was back at the door with a satisfied smile on her face.

"That's the man who was parked out in front of my place yesterday. I don't like the looks of him at all. I choose him as the bad one." Sophia moved over to Granger and looked him up and down. "This one, I trust. Yes, I knocked on his window, but I like his face. But that's just me."

Bailey stared at the man seated in the chair. She knew she was in way over her head and like it or not, she was going to have to call A.J. on this one.

"Sophia, would you dial this number for me and hand me the phone when they answer?"

Sophia had a phone in her kitchen that was bright yellow – her favorite color – and a cord long enough to take it anywhere in the kitchen she wanted to go. Bailey called out the numbers never taking her eyes off the man.

"This is Sophia, Bailey, she tell me to call you. Hold on."

Sophia handed the phone to Bailey and when she heard A.J.'s gruff "What's this about?" she physically relaxed.

"Okay, here's the deal. I have some man at gunpoint here in Sophia's kitchen and another one tied up beside the garage. How soon can you get here?"

Everyone in the kitchen heard the shout coming from the receiver, "What!!!"

Bailey pulled the phone away from her ear, shook her head and tried to stop the ringing. She took a deep breath and repeated what she had said. Once the cursing stopped and Bailey could get a word in, A.J. finally agreed to be there as fast as he could. Luckily, he wasn't on assignment. He didn't live that far away, so said he could make it in 15 minutes. Could she hang in that long or should he call the police for backup?

Chapter Fifty-Six

Bailey looked across the table at the man staring back at her. He was lounging in the chair as though there wasn't a woman holding a gun on him and said 15 minutes would be fine. She felt between her gun and Sophia's baseball bat, they could do a lot of damage if he moved. Her bigger concern was the lout out by the garage. Sophia explained that wouldn't be a problem. She had given him a little tap in the head when he started stirring after she nudged him with her foot.

Bailey shook her head and the man's eyes widened. He let a little smile escape and then stopped when he saw her eyes narrow at him. Like she was just daring him to think this was funny.

"So, who are you anyway?" she asked.

"My name is Granger Williams. I'm a private investigator from Los Angeles. I was sent here on assignment to follow Carl Younger. I lost track of him at Golden Gate Park and then you came into the picture. Bailey, why do you have a gun?"

"I have a permit. Wait a minute, how do you know my name?"

"I'm a private detective; I detect."

Bailey was trying not to shoot this smart aleck just on principle, but she needed more information. Granger was too smooth and too comfortable sitting here in Sophia's kitchen. It was like he was enjoying the situation a little too much. And he was too much the epitome of a "private detective" or "private dick." Just the type she'd been fighting against ever since she got her license, and now here he was besting her on her own case – her first case. Bailey shook her head. She just wanted this to all be over. She had to figure out what was so important in those papers that someone was willing to kill for it and then come after her.

Just then, A.J. pushed through the door.

"What did you do, run every red light?"

"Just those where no one else was coming." A.J. looked the "prisoner" up and down, saw he was relaxed in the chair and then said to him, "Are you going to explain what's going on? How'd you let her get the drop on you anyway?" A.J. smirked.

"Hey!" Bailey exclaimed. "Really? That's your first question?"

"Don't get your panties in a twist. If he could take down that muscle out by the garage – yeah, I checked him out first – then I'm trying to figure out how you surprised him. He doesn't look that easy to surprise."

"I've been on high alert ever since this whole case started. There's no insulation between the garage and my apartment. I guess I just felt someone there. And I guess my instincts were right, because there he is," she said with satisfaction.

A.J. pushed Bailey's gun-arm down and she took a deep breath. She felt like she had been holding it for two days.

"Okay, let's get the 'niceties' out of the way. Who are you and what are you doing here?" A.J. said.

Chapter Fifty-Seven

Granger let out a sigh, "My name is Granger Williams and I'm a private investigator hired to track Carl Younger and to see what he was up to. Lost track of him after leaving the airport and later learned he was dead. Not a good result on my part. Wasn't sure how Bailey was involved, but when I caught our 'friend' out there tailing her, I decided she might need some protection."

Bailey raised her gun again after Granger stopped talking. If A.J. hadn't been there she might have followed her gut reaction and shot him right between those blue eyes. The fact that she had needed protection galled her even more.

There they were: Bailey, A.J., Sophia and this Granger character. It was time to figure things out. The answer was in those papers otherwise that gorilla out there wouldn't have been so anxious to take her out.

"Let's take a look at those papers Younger gave you and see where we are in this mess," A.J. said.

Bailey led the way up to her apartment. It was even more crowded once everyone made their way in. There was no place to sit and the walls were covered with the paper bags Bailey had taped up earlier.

A.J. forgot about the "confidentially" part he'd told Bailey before. Her life had been in danger and now was not the time to let something like that get in the way.

"Lots of figures and companies, but what makes this worth killing for?"

"It's filled with inconsistencies and shell company after shell company. Some of these only exist on paper. Carl had the thread, he just didn't know the players that well. I think that's why he asked Peter to hire someone who was local and could 'pull the curtain back' so to speak. And Peter recommended me."

Bailey walked over to the freezer and removed the files she had been working from.

"That gives a whole new meaning for keeping something 'on ice", A.J. said.

A.J. and Bailey nodded at each other. "Yep, time to call Peter. Whatever is hiding in there, he'll help uncover."

Bailey dialed Peter's number. He didn't pick up so she left a message saying to get over to her place as soon as he received the message. "It's a life or death situation." Peter knew that Bailey wasn't big on drama and would take it with the seriousness warranted.

In the meantime, there was the man by the garage that had to be dealt with.

"I think it's time we asked our trussed-up man some questions while we wait for Peter to arrive," said A.J.

He then pushed his way through the group, motioned for Granger to follow and they went downstairs to the garage.

"Well! Aren't they just the best of buddies?" Bailey said.

"I tell you. He has a good face," said Sophia whispered.

Chapter Fifty-Eight

A.J. and Granger loosened the ropes around their hostage so that he could walk and dragged him into Sophia's kitchen. He was still groggy so A.J. splashed water in his face from the sink, causing him to sputter and he jerked his head up. His eyes were still out of focus so Granger slapped him on the face to bring him around.

Theo opened his eyes and saw two men staring at him. Hey, one of them was the guy who had cut him off on the freeway coming over here this afternoon. God, his head hurt. He tried to rub it, but his hands were tied behind his back. Okay, this wasn't good, this wasn't good at all. He had failed this contract in the worst way possible. A man was dead, he didn't have the papers and now he was trussed up like a Thanksgiving turkey. It was just a question of how much they knew or thought they knew.

This whole time, he was moving his head slowly from one of the men to the other. They were too relaxed. What did they know? They never said a word. Just stared at him. He started to squirm.

"Okay. So, what's this all about? Huh?" Theo asked.

"Why don't you tell us? And then we'll tell you whether we believe you or not. Start with your name," A.J. reached behind him and produced the gun Granger had taken from Theo. "This yours?"

Theo paled. He had stupidly kept the gun. It'd been his "good luck charm" in many a contract, but this time it could cost him everything. If they matched it to the slug they pulled out of that accountant, he was definitely cooked. Okay, maybe a little spin on the truth.

"It's Theo. Hey. So yeah, I was following the guy. But he tried to be a hero, grabbed at me. All I wanted was the papers. He should of just given them to me. How'd I know he'd grab for the gun. It was his fault. I was just defending myself."

"Really? That's the story? Then why dump his body in the Bay?" Granger asked.

"So I screwed up," Theo said, "Last time I take a contract outside New York or Jersey," Theo muttered.

Yeah, like I'll get another chance after this mess Theo thought to himself.

Theo felt the sweat start to gather on his forehead and under his armpits. He was always the one in control. He was the one making his victim sweat. He didn't like the way this felt at all.

"I'll be lucky to just go to jail. Staying alive inside will be harder than staying alive outside. The man who hired me has too much pull."

Theo felt he had only one bargaining chip left: maybe he could make a deal and reveal who hired him.

If that girl really had the papers, well, that would be the proof, right? Theo thought.

Chapter Fifty-Nine

Bailey came rushing into the kitchen holding a stack of the papers. "I've got it! I know who's behind all this!"

Theo slumped in his chair.

Bailey spread out the papers on the counter. She wasn't going anywhere near that man without a gun or Sophia's baseball bat.

"It's right here! See? Notice whose name keeps coming up? Andrew Nelson."

When Bailey said the name "Nelson," Theo knew she didn't have a clue. Maybe there was still a chance that he could bargain his way out of this.

She pointed to the name of the shell company she had researched at the County office. God, was that only three days ago? She put her notes next to the papers she'd gotten from Carl and there was the proof. It had been hidden in a memo attached to the audit that Carl Younger had done.

Bailey knew Andrew Nelson. He'd been to dinners at the house with the Judge. They sat on the same board of the San Francisco Opera Society. This just seemed to be out of character for what she knew of the man. There had to be something else going on, but it was his name that kept popping up.

"Is that who hired you, Nelson?" A.J. questioned.

"Don't know anybody called that," Theo answered and relaxed as he said it. That response and movement couldn't have been a bigger giveaway.

Bailey turned around and looked at Theo. Their only ace in this game was sitting right in front of them. He was the thread that would cause this whole scheme to unravel. Bailey looked at A.J. and Granger.

"What do you think? Can we hook the big fish? Looks like we have some tasty bait." Bailey truly smiled and took a deep breath for the first time since her meeting at Golden Gate Park.

They had to figure out a way to get to Nelson, and right now, maybe Peter was their way in. And then they'd bait the hook and find out what was really going on here.

Chapter Sixty

They heard a car screech to a halt in the driveway and then a car door slam shut. Bailey hurried to the Sophia's kitchen door just as Peter was turning toward the stairs to Bailey's place.

"Peter, we're in here."

Peter turned from where he was climbing the stairs and hurried back to Sophia's house.

"Are you okay?? What's going on?"

"We have a situation. Breathe, I've got A.J. and Sophia in the kitchen along with a few uninvited guests."

Peter and Bailey entered the kitchen together. Granger sensed that same air of intimacy that he had seen through the window the first night he followed Bailey. He didn't like how it made him feel. He nodded at Peter and then glanced at A.J. to do the introductions.

Peter's head swiveled to the man tied up in the chair and turned back to Bailey with a quizzical look.

"Peter," A.J. said, "Here's the long and short of it. The guy tied up shot Younger, then came after Bailey to get the papers he was supposed to get from him. This other guy is a PI from Los Angeles, Granger Williams, who was also following Younger."

"Okay," Peter said as he sat down on the stool by the counter.

"Peter, I think we've begun to make sense of the paperwork Carl entrusted to me. He was right, he knew something wasn't kosher, but he didn't have the local knowledge or access to the same information I could get. He started me on the search and I followed with my investigation at the County Records office, but here's the thing." Bailey pulled out the papers she had been going through and a memo that Carl had attached to the back of one of his papers. It looked like it had been stapled in error because it was facing backward and didn't have the careful preparation that all the other papers had.

"Are you seeing what I see?" Bailey asked Peter.

Peter began going through the papers she had separated into piles. He stopped every once in a while, and then went back and look again. After he finished, he sat down, hard, on the stool.

"This is a mess," Peter said. "I know Andrew Nelson. I can't see how he'd be involved in this level of corruption or attempted theft let alone murder."

"Accidental murder," Theo said defensively.

"It speaks," Peter said.

"Here's the thing, Peter. This lout over here doesn't know the name Nelson, so there's some other player, someone pulling the strings. Can you think of who?"

Peter glanced back at the papers on the counter. "It's nine o'clock. Let me call Andrew."

Chapter Sixty-One

"What! Are you crazy? What are you going to say, 'Oh, by the way, Andrew, we have proof that you're up to your eyeballs in illegal dealings?' You can't take those papers to him!"

"Bailey, I said 'call,' not take them to him."

Peter looked at her. "Really? Bailey, you know I don't forget anything I've heard or read. Your papers are safe here with you. I just need to get some answers before anyone else gets hurt."

"I won't be leaving here until I know she's safe," A.J. said.

"Me, too," said Granger

"Me, also," said Sophia as she fondled her baseball bat.

"Where can we get him to come where he won't be suspicious? It can't be at the office."

Bailey looked at Peter and said, "Then it has to be at the Judge's. Let me call Marge and see if the Judge has a case tomorrow. If he's gone all day then we're in the clear. Andrew won't suspect anything if we meet him there."

Peter looked at Bailey and said, "You know I can't be there, right? I would be jeopardizing the whole thing and the confidentially of other clients that might be involved."

As she dialed the familiar number, Bailey thought about what the Judge would say if he knew what she had planned. He was a "law and order" judge and he wouldn't tolerate anyone bending the law. She held her breath until Marge answered the phone.

"Marge? Hey it's Bailey. What's the Judge's schedule tomorrow? There's a book I need from the library and I'm not in any mood for his third degree." Bailey listened and nodded to Peter and the others, "I see. A high-profile case. Hmm, got it, out all day. Thanks, Marge. I'll phone you when I'm on my way.

"Peter, it's time to call Andrew and set this plan in motion."

Peter took the receiver from Bailey and dialed Nelson's number. He answered after only a few rings. He explained that there was a meeting scheduled at the Judge's house tomorrow and could he be there at 10.

Chapter Sixty-Two

"All set. Now, what do we do with the muscle until then?" They looked at each other and Sophia said, "You leave him with me." Theo sat back in his chair staring at the woman with the bat. "And me," A.J. said.

A.J., Granger and Peter took Theo to the basement and secured him to the hooks that Sophia used to cure her hams for her famous prosciutto. There was a bathroom, so the group suggested he make use of it while he could.

No one left the house that night. They had to figure out a plan to get the information they needed from Andrew. Sophia made several pots of thick, dark coffee and they planned until the morning.

Peter left early on and Sophia cooked up some eggs and ham for those remaining. She even took some down to Theo. She wanted him in good shape for what they had planned.

A.J. and Bailey weren't thrilled with the arrangement, but Sophia had protection and Bailey would be able to tell if there was any collusion with Granger and Andrew Nelson. They left for the Judge's at about 9:15 – after the commute traffic and safely after the Judge left for his case. Bailey phoned ahead just to be sure he was gone and also that her mom was at her weekly Women of the Arts association meeting. Coast clear, their plan was a go.

When Bailey rang the doorbell, Marge smiled at Bailey and then looked over at the man with her. "You need help to find a book?"

"Sorry, Marge, but it's really important that we use the library and we're expecting someone else. When Andrew Nelson arrives will you tell him the Judge is expecting him and show him into the library?"

"Well, if you had told me were we having a party, I would have prepared some tea and crumpets," she harrumphed away.

Chapter Sixty-Three

Bailey and Granger had brought along a stack of papers that looked very similar to the ones Bailey had gotten from Younger. Peter was pretty sure that Andrew wouldn't know the difference – just papers with numbers and names.

The doorbell rang again. It was show time as they heard Marge say, "Yes the Judge is expecting you in the library. Let me show you the way."

"Oh, hello, Bailey, I didn't know you'd be here. Where is the Judge?" Andrew asked.

"He won't be joining us. In fact, considering what I have to say, he'd probably be the last person you would want in this room right now."

"Bailey, what's with all the dramatics? And who's this person? If the Judge isn't here, I'll be leaving." Andrew turned toward the door.

"Sit down, Andrew. Do you recognize these papers? They are the papers produced for your proposed merger."

"And?"

"And, I think the SEC would be quite interested in these other filings we found."

Andrew grabbed ahold of the back of the cracked leather chair just inside the library. Then he lowered himself down onto the worn cushion.

"And what do you think you have?"

"Possible fraud and murder."

"Murder? Are you nuts? What murder? Who's been murdered?"

Granger tilted his head and looked at the man seated in front of him. He seemed really perplexed.

"What's going on here?"

Bailey said, "We have proof that you have hidden assets inside shell corporations you've set up, Andrew. That proof was partially verified by the accounting firm that was hired to review the documents; an accounting firm in Los Angeles. And that accountant was found dead in the Bay the other day."

"Oh, my God! No, this can't be happening! It's all his fault! It's all HIS fault! Murder? I had nothing to do with murder!"

Andrew covered his face and started rocking back and forth. “I’ll tell you everything! Everything! I may go to prison for fraud, but not before I put that son-of-a-bitch in jail first.”

The others pulled up a chairs and Andrew told them his story.

Chapter Sixty-Four

"I headed Swift Investments, I know, stupid name, it was homage to my late uncle who first got me involved in investing. It wasn't until after the name had been approved by the Security and Exchange Commission that I made the connection. People called me a "rainmaker" because I could generate more clients in one hour then most investment bankers could in one month. I was proud that my returns were phenomenal, and my client list was exclusive, containing only those with referrals from other clients having a net worth on over $1 million."

Andrew smiled, "I was known as the "golden boy," I didn't want to give away my secrets. I kept them close to my vest and left my clients begging for more.

"I admit I was obsessed with the rich and powerful and I didn't always vet my clients as well as I should have. Case in point: Anthony Sabana."

Granger and Bailey looked at each other quizzically when they heard the name, "Sabana" and started to interrupt, but Andrew wasn't finished.

"It was that attorney, Stan McKinney, who introduced us three years ago and was confident we would be 'good' for each other.

"Sabana owned a large construction company, processing plants: one for concrete and one for asphalt and a heavy equipment leasing company. He was not my target client. I preferred independently wealthy complete with family monies. I was surprised when McKinney brought him to one of my gatherings at my place in Napa."

Andrew explained that he didn't know McKinney that well, but David Gleason, McKinney's law partner, had been a client since he opened his business and was responsible for many of the "A" list clients he had, so I couldn't really deny Gleason's partner, McKinney, access nor his associate, Sabana.

Andrew said, "I remember that first conversation word for word." And recited it to Bailey and Granger. They both listened intently as Andrew told his story.

Chapter Sixty-Five

Stan McKinney introduced Sabana to Andrew, he told Bailey and Granger, at a wine-tasting event he was hosting, and Sabana got right to the point.

"So, what's it gonna take to buy into this "Swift Investment" that everybody's been talking about?" Sabana asked.

"I think you misunderstood today's event," I grimaced at McKinney. "This is a wine tasting to raise funds for the arts, a *social* event; I won't be doing any business today."

Andrew remembered Sabana's shrug. "I don't know any *businessman* who doesn't take every opportunity to do *business*. Even when my grandfather invited the priests for dinner, it was to get them to commit to his painting their frescos before the last sip of wine. Oh, yes, I have an appreciation for the arts, but I have more of an appreciation for money. Without *money*, this event would be meaningless." With that comment, Sabana turned and walked away.

"I was stunned," Andrew said.

"Stan McKinney watched Sabana walk away and then leaned into me, 'You do not want to make that man your enemy.'"

Andrew face flushed red as he still recalled how furious he'd been.

"I asked McKinney, 'What were you thinking by bringing him here?'

"'Remember, everybody's money is green and even the wealthiest "old money" families started with a little dirt on their hands,'" McKinney retorted.

"Just then a waiter came by with a fresh tray of wineglasses to sample, McKinney took one that was offered, sipped it as he left, 'Nice vintage, Andrew.'"

"That was my first meeting."

Chapter Sixty-Six

Andrew got up from the chair in the Judge's library and started to pace. It was obvious that he had needed to tell somebody what happened. The words came spewing out.

"In the days that followed, I did a little bit of discrete checking on Mr. Anthony Sabana. His family had been in San Francisco since the early 1900s. They originally came from the Palermo region of Italy and migrated to this country in the 1880s to New York and then out to San Francisco. Sabana was, indeed, a patron of the arts and owned a beautiful Beaux Arts home near the Bay.

"I couldn't get any deeper insights, because everyone I talked to was pretty tight-lipped about Sabana and had only glowing things to say, when they would speak at all."

Andrew kept spewing out his story.

"A week passed and I was pushing to get some trades committed before the closing bell, when my secretary buzzed through saying she had a Mr. Sabana on the line, and would I take the call. I wanted to tell him to get lost, but that caution that Stan McKinney whispered in my ear put a chill up my spine." Andrew turned to Bailey and Granger looking for some sort of support.

"I just knew I couldn't put this guy off," Andrew said.

Andrew was trying to justify his actions, his fear toward Sabana. Bailey understood the implications. She'd seen men like that try to play the Judge, but he wouldn't have any of it, although she knew how formidable they could be.

"After that, it was all downhill. Before I knew it, we had set up an appointment. I felt like I had made a deal with the devil."

Chapter Sixty-Seven

Andrew pushed his hair out of his face and then sank into the chair again. "You've got to understand. He came with a cashier's check for $1.2 million dollars!" Andrew licked the sweat off his upper lip.

"And he took all my recommendations, so I thought it'd be okay.

"Then a year ago, everything came off the rails. Sabana stopped taking my advice and wanted his monies invested in funds that he had picked and became very hands-on in his approach.

"A month into this new process, I scheduled an appointment to see if I could get this back under control. Sabana sat back in his chair, crossed his leg, took his time lighting up a very expensive cigar, and then looked me directly in the eye.

"'What percentage do you make on my account each month?'

"The industry standard on a portfolio this size is 1.5%." I pointed it out on the statement.

"Sabana puffed on his cigar, sat forward in his chair and said, 'Let me understand our relationship. I give you my money and you invest it, correct? Then I watch my money grow and you take your percentage each month, correct?'

"I nodded my head. 'So why should you care if I tell you *where* I want my money? You invest it and you *still* make money. It's my money, my choices.'

"I tried to make him understand, but Sabana held up his hand, effectively stopping me from continuing.

"'I think you were listening, but not *hearing* me. It's my money. You just do what I tell you and everything will be fine. You make money; I make money and if I lose money, that's on me, got it?'"

Andrew said, "I thought everything would be okay if I just let him do what he wanted. I'd invite him to fund-raisers, like all my other clients, but he always refused."

Andrew looked at the window as he continued, "I'd see Sabana around San Francisco. He had box seats at the opera and ballet, attended major art exhibits, was generous with his patronage to new and struggling artists, even attended Forty-Niner games at Kezar Stadium on occasion, but even after all these years there was that veiled threat of violence in his every movement and comment."

Chapter Sixty-Eight

Bailey asked, "Why didn't you just give him back his money?"

Granger shook his head. "Not possible. Once a barracuda like that gets his money in your business, it's all downhill from there."

"Right? You know what I mean, right?" Andrew turned to Granger.

Andrew stood in front of Granger and addressed him directly. "So, you can imagine my surprise when I was *told,* not asked, by Anthony Sabana that he had arranged the sale of my business to Allan and Sons, a long-time competitor.

"The announcement came through Stan McKinney and was presented a fait accompli, no input, nothing! I couldn't believe the audacity of the man. What about my clientele that I had meticulously cultivated over the years? What about that? It was my company, damn it - mine!"

Andrew ran his fingers through his hair, further mussing it.

"I told McKinney to get lost and take Sabana with him. It was my name on the filings, my name registered with the SEC! My name and reputation that imbibed the business I had built from nothing."

Bailey moved over to Andrew and walked him back to the chair.

This recitation by Andrew allowed Granger and Bailey to see the strain he was under, but still not what had led to theft and murder.

Andrew seemed to be swallowed up by the chair, a much smaller man that the one who had walked in so assuredly a short time ago.

Andrew was talking so quietly, that Granger and Bailey had to move closer to hear him.

"Stan McKinney sat in the same chair Anthony Sabana had, folded his hands and said, 'Exactly.'

"'What am I missing here? You agree with everything I just said, so what am I missing?'

"'It is your name on everything, and if your files were opened by a SEC investigation, they would find investments in some very dubious companies, some of which, it seems, don't even exist.'"

Chapter Sixty-Nine

Even saying those words brought tears to Andrew's eyes. He looked up at them. "This had been the plan from the beginning. Meticulously played, month after month until the trap was so complete, I had no way out. How could I have been so stupid? My fate was sealed from that first meeting when I had cavalierly pushed Sabana aside as a nobody."

"I take it, it was this McKinney's idea to have a Los Angeles accounting firm look at the paperwork for the takeover?" asked Bailey.

"Yeah. He said they wouldn't look at it too carefully and then of all things they assign this "by the book" accountant who is so detail-oriented and started asking questions that Sabana and McKinney didn't want asked."

Andrew's eyes grew wide, "But hey, I didn't know anything about a murder! I haven't had any contact with either of them once the paperwork was submitted. I was told I'd be told when to show up to sign the documents before they were recorded."

"You haven't asked," Granger said, "but my involvement in this whole thing is that I'm a private investigator hired by Allan and Sons. They wanted to know what the delay was on the audit prior to the purchase. Allan's no fool. He couldn't figure out why your firm was suddenly for sale."

Bailey looked at Granger, "So we really were working on the same case, just from different angles?"

"Exactly."

"But," Andrew whined, "That still doesn't get me out of this mess." When Andrew had first walked into the library that morning, his charcoal grey pin-striped suit and white shirt with a black silk tie made him look in control. Now he was disheveled, and his suit was wrinkled from his squirming.

Bailey looked at Granger and nodded. "We may have a little insurance policy. We actually have the murderer in our possession."

"Have you called the cops? You have no idea how deep Sabana's control goes in this city. I'm sure there are cops, even captains on his payroll. You don't get as rich as he is by doing things by the book. I'm living proof," Andrew sputtered.

"No worries," Granger said, "One of my pals from the Marine Corps is a cop here. I'm not sure what precinct, but he's straight as an arrow and I would trust him with my life. Did in Vietnam.

"We just need to figure out a place to meet where the goon Sabana hired can do a bit of acting and get him to reveal himself. Do you think Sabana will fall for it?" Granger asked

"He's pretended to keep his hands clean, but I think that's only the white-collar stuff. From what I've seen of him and heard through the grapevine, he doesn't mind getting in the middle of something if he thinks it'll prove a point. And this sounds just like that situation," Andrew said.

Chapter Seventy

"I'll contact Mac and we'll arrange to have everything in place this evening. Where would he meet someone where he'd feel in control?"

"His concrete plant. I'm sure there has been more than one person end up in the foundation of one of San Francisco's finest establishments."

Granger pulled out his battered notebook and leafed through the papers until he found Mac's name and number. He picked up the phone on the Judge's desk and dialed.

Granger explained the problem and Mac started laughing, "Well, brother, you finally come to my city and you step in it big time. I guess I'm going to have to save your butt like I did in Nam. You know you're going to owe me big time, right?"

"Hey, buddy, if this is half the case I think it is you could be wearing those sergeant bars quicker than you thought."

They both shared a laugh and Granger gave him the address where the meet would take place that evening.

Chapter Seventy-One

It was dark early in the evening that time of year, so any reconnaissance had to be sooner rather than later. It may not have been the jungles of Vietnam, but it was unknown territory to Granger and *known* territory to this Sabana character. Now they had to get Theo to play his part.

Andrew said, "I can't go home! What if I was followed or something? I'm not a good actor. I know I'd give something away."

Bailey suggested that he follow them back to her place and wait with her landlady until everything was over. Andrew's face relaxed.

They all left the house together and Marge came out of the kitchen and said, "So, I'm not mentioning this to your mom or the Judge, right?"

"Thanks, Marge. I promise I'll explain everything tomorrow. No need to worry anybody."

"Oh, sure, except me!"

"Trust me, she'll be okay," Granger said.

"I don't even know you, why should I trust anything you say?" Marge glowered.

Bailey leaned in and gave Marge a big hug and held on a little longer than usual. That didn't seem to reassure Marge at all. She pulled away and looked her right in the eye.

"You be careful! Something tells me that if this goes wrong, a Band-Aid won't fix it."

Did she think everything would work out? This was not how she envisioned her first case at all. But, if she wanted to prove herself in this world, she had to toughen up, and for all the testosterone around her, if they thought she was going to sit this one out, they didn't know her at all. She had a gun and she knew how to use it. This all started with her and it would end with her.

They went back to Sophia's and made sure Theo was still in place, then gathered around Sophia's table to work out the logistics for that night.

A.J., Granger and Bailey met Granger's friend Mac at a local diner near the concrete plant. They watched the comings and goings and found out there was only an over-sized shed that was used as an office. Because it was winter, the plant closed early once the temperatures dropped too much to make deliveries. It wasn't lit well, only one light over the office and one spotlight that illuminated the small warehouse where the supplies were kept.

The place was surrounded by wire fencing and there were limited places someone could hide. All in all it was a better place for Sabana than for them. Someone was going to have to stay there and wait until Sabana arrived and see if he brought any backup with him. Mac knew the area, so he was put on watch while the others went back to get Theo, the false papers, and to convince Theo that his only chance out of this without a first-degree murder charge was to do what they said.

Chapter Seventy-Two

Granger went back to his motel to change into some dark clothing and get extra ammunition in case things got dicey. He could tell by the set of Bailey's jaw that there was no talking her into staying behind.

Granger checked with Mac to see if there were any others on the force that could be trusted with the night's mission

"I love my guys, Granger, but the pay is low and these guys have families. There aren't many that I could say would be straight enough. Probably keeping it to just us is a good idea. Later, I can radio in the takedown and get backup, but for now, this is a small operation."

Granger knew what he was saying. It was a problem in a lot of police forces. Times were hard.

A.J. and Bailey had changed into darker clothing as well. Sophia was not happy to be saddled with this wimp, as she called Andrew, and miss out on all the action. She tapped her baseball bat against her hand just in case that guy tried to warn anyone. The kitchen was tense with the distrust between them. *Glad she had moved her gun into her apron pocket*, Sophia thought.

A.J. and Granger brought Theo up from the basement.

"Do you understand what you are supposed to say when you call Sabana?"

Theo shrugged, "Yeah, like I have a choice in this. Play the role or go to jail for murder. Some pick."

"My buddy was a sharpshooter in the military, so I'm telling you ahead of time, he'll have his sights on you and if you so much as twitch the wrong way, jail won't be an option."

Bailey handed Theo the phone. He dialed the check-in number he was given.

"Hey, it's me. Yeah, well you didn't tell me the guy was built like a linebacker. I never expected him to grab the gun. Calm down. I had to make sure I wasn't followed before I brought the papers to you. No, I didn't read them. I don't need to know what it says. I want to meet in the open. You still got that concrete plant? Okay, at 7 then. Anybody else going to be there? Right, see you then and you'd better have the rest of my money. I am out of Dodge and on the first plane home. If I'd known what was coming I would have charged more."

"Satisfied?" Theo said as Bailey hung up the phone.

Granger and Bailey had listened in as Theo made the call. Sabana didn't seem fazed by the request to meet at the concrete plant. Of course, they didn't think that Sabana had any intention of letting Theo walk out of there after he got the papers. At least, that's what they were counting on. Everything that Andrew had told them seemed to reveal that. And Mac had told Granger that Sabana had been on the corruption task force's radar for many years, but they could never get any real dirt or find anyone who was willing to testify. That was about to change.

Chapter Seventy-Three

Theo drove his car to the meeting place. A.J. was scrunched down in the back seat. There was no way they were letting him out of their sight. A.J. had his gun pointed directly at Theo's back. Theo could actually feel it through the back cushion – or at least he thought he could. This was a very unusual position for him to be in – he had always been the intimidator, but everything about this job was anything but ordinary.

Theo slowed down as he approached the concrete plant. He glanced around but didn't see any other cars parked nearby. He pulled over along the dirt bank next to the entrance to wait and see if Sabana would actually show up.

Sweat was gathering on Theo's lip and he moved his hand quickly to wipe it away. It wouldn't do anyone any good if he looked less than completely confident. His only way out of this was to get Sabana to say something or make a move, something that he hoped he wouldn't do.

Suddenly, headlights appeared around the corner. It was a large black Chrysler. Theo wasn't sure if Sabana had his driver with him, but as the car approached, there was only one silhouette backlit by the streetlight at the end of the road. Of course, that didn't mean that someone wasn't slouched down in back just like he had. Timing would be everything with this.

Granger and Bailey had positioned themselves behind a dumpster to the side of the office. They had come in early screened by a large cement truck that was coming back from a run. They had instructed Theo to pull his car up so that it shielded them from view and they could be ready if Sabana made a move.

The big black Chrysler rolled up to the gate, Sabana got out, unlocked it, returned to his car and pulled inside, right where Granger and Bailey were waiting. Not the plan.

Theo whispered, "Now what?"

A.J. said, "Pull in facing his car so that the headlights shine onto his car. That way neither of you is too vulnerable. Granger and Bailey can still move in behind your vehicle with a line of sight to Sabana."

As soon as Granger and Bailey saw what had occurred and before Granger could stop her, Bailey ran around to the other side of the office, just where the shadow from the light hid her from view. She knew she had to have a clear line of sight to Sabana. In case he came armed there was no way she could overpower him. She knew her limits – she'd leave that job to Granger. He seemed more than capable in that department. The most important thing was to hear what was being said and keep Theo safe, so he could testify. They needed to nail this guy to the wall.

Bailey slid down until she was prone in the shadows and edged nearer where the two cars were parked.

Sabana got out of the car and Theo followed. They stood facing each other.

Chapter Seventy-Four

"You got my papers?" Sabana asked.

"Sure do." Theo held up a folder that they had given him. "How we gonna work this? I feel like we're in a hostage exchange; me for the papers."

A huge grin spread across Sabana's face, but with the shadows from the overhead lamp and the bluish tint of the bulb, it looked sinister.

"Those are my property so hand them over. If they check out, you get your money."

Theo bent down and slid them over to him, the folder kicking up dust as it moved.

Sabana bent over and picked them up and at the same time reached into his boot and pulled out a revolver secreted in an ankle hoister and raised it up pointing at Theo.

Theo froze and then all hell broke loose. Granger and Bailey came out with their guns drawn and Mac took a shot from his perch that caused the gun to fly out of Sabana's hand and he recoiled with a yell.

A.J. came out of the back door and grabbed Sabana and pulled his arms behind his back.

"You're a dead man, Theo," Sabana seethed. "There's no place safe for you. I'll see to that."

Granger heard Mac radio in the call for 'officer needs assistance' as soon as Mac put down his rifle and he saw that the others had the situation in control. Theo had turned to run, but Bailey hit him behind the knees with the baton she had trained with but never had the opportunity to use in a real life situation. She smiled as she watched Theo writhing on the ground. Yep, that was going to smart.

Granger used the office telephone to call Peter and tell him to let Detective Kwok know that the suspect they had been looking for in the murder was in custody and could be found at the local precinct.

Chapter Seventy-Five

It wasn't easily explained to the Captain that Mac had been involved in an unauthorized stakeout, but once the anti-corruption task force of the FBI was notified, they smoothed things over. The FBI had been looking for inside information on Sabana's operations for years. Theo's best chance of survival was to cooperate. He did know where all the "bodies" were buried. Granger thought it wouldn't be long before Mac was tagged for bigger things.

The FBI were tasked with financial crimes and those papers Bailey had were a gold mine of information.

After all their statements had been made and with clearance from Detective Kwok, Granger and Bailey headed back to Sophia's place to see how she was faring with Andrew and report on the evening's results. It was a quiet ride. Neither Granger nor Bailey knew what to say. They were unwilling accomplices. He knew more about her then she knew about him. After all, he had been following her around for the past couple of days. But Bailey didn't know him at all. The others were ready to trust him, but she was slower in that department. Yes, A.J. had made phone calls prior to the night's stakeout to verify his story and yes, it did check out, but there was something unsettling to Bailey.

"You're pretty quiet over there," Granger finally said.

"I'm relieved it's over, but this was my first case and I couldn't even do it by myself."

"Bailey, the sign of a good PI is knowing when to accept help. We couldn't have managed all this tonight if we hadn't had help from so many people. Strength is knowing when you can rely on others that may have more experience. As you gain more, you'll be better able to assist others, too. You scared the daylights out of me when you took off around that office shed. But I had to trust you or I couldn't have done what I needed to do. Do you understand?"

Bailey nodded and looked out the car window. She smiled. Yeah, just wait until the next case.

THE END

About the Author

Linda Lynch-Johnson is an international best-selling author and a master storyteller.

Her life history has taught her the power of listening. She says, "You never know where your next story idea will come from, you have to listen for it."

Linda is the author of a children's book, *Marcis and the Rainmaker, Perspective: A Collection of Short Stories*, and is contributing author to *365 Moment of Grace* and *Contemporary Earth Design: A Feng Shui Anthology* and has caused her friends to call her "The Librarian of Health and Hope."

Her book, *The Adapter Factor: When Change Scares the Hell Out of You*, which features her Adapter Factor methods, has created a new understanding in dealing with change.

She is a popular presenter at conferences throughout the United States and the world on the subject of change

For more information, please visit her website: lindalynchjohnson.com

Linda's books are available with links to Amazon.com and from Barnes and Noble and other major booksellers.

Made in the USA
San Bernardino, CA
15 October 2018